D1621203

Black Faces, White Faces

Black Faces, White Faces

JANE GARDAM

for Julia
best of all editors.
Kindest & best of friends.
from
Jane.

HAMISH HAMILTON
LONDON

First published in Great Britain 1975
by Hamish Hamilton Ltd
90 Great Russell Street London WC1B 3PT

Copyright © 1975 by Jane Gardam

SBN 241 89250 3

The quotation on page 97 is from *The Collected Poems*
1965 by Robert Graves and is reprinted by permission
of Robert Graves

Printed in Great Britain by
Bristol Typesetting Co. Ltd
Barton Manor St Philips Bristol

For Sandy Gully

Contents

'I own . . . that if landscapes were sold one penny plain and twopence coloured, I should go to the length of twopence every day of my life.'

Robert Louis Stevenson
Travels with a Donkey

I   *Babe Jude*

The lady lay in a little glen—if bananas and coconuts and catstails and fire-of-the-forest and heat can make a cool-sounding thing like a glen—and from under thick lids examined Mrs Filling who stood on the sand at the glen's edge with the sharp, green Caribbean sea behind her.

Mrs Filling wore a hat and carried a handbag. She had drawn the line at stockings (ninetyish in the glen's shade) and her dress had only holes where the arms might be, like everyone else's dress, and there were only sandals on her feet. But Sunday was Sunday, the Anglican Church the Anglican Church even at Pineapple Bay, and Matins Matins. Let Henry go off in the glass-bottomed boat in his bathing trunks, she and the Jamaicans were for prayer books and careful clothes.

She had walked back down the empty main street of Pineapple Bay under the shouting sun with rivers trickling down her back and running down her arms and legs, back to the great, cool hotel with its ageing rich Americans sipping rum punch under the colonnade, to tell Henry about the service. She felt tired and rather faint.

And Henry was not there. Not in their room, not on their verandah, not on the terraces and now, down by the burning steps to the sea, not on the private beach. 'He's out in the glass-bottomed boat, Ma'am,' they said by the jetty. 'That's maybe where he gone, Ma'am. Out over on the reef.' And they watched her as she went, heavy-footed in

A*

the soft sand, carrying her handbag, sinewy from knee to ankle. They noted the hump above the shoulder-blades, the hump of age, the hump acknowledged now in dress-making, the hump that stills desire. 'First the waist,' she had been thinking in church, looking at the tall and careless Jamaican backs in the pew in front. 'The waist gets high. You adapt the pattern. Then the length. You drop the hem. You cover the heavy, rounded part above each knee-cap. Then this rising hump at the nape of the neck. But you can't cover the box jaw, the lines, the sagging chin. And afterwards the cords in the hands, the fat ankles, the brown spots on the arms. Then real age—the slow, flat-footed step, the groping hands, red rings to the eyes, thin hair, uncertain heart and head. Sex and all that sort of thing so lost that it isn't even the memory . . .' Mrs Filling stumbled in the thick white sand. 'Where am I?'

She had walked across the private beach, newly raked, deserted. White tables under their umbrellas were deserted, the sea empty, not a wave stirring, and at the end of the beach had come to the glade and the woman, large as a fallen tree, draped in a silky lilac dressing-gown, flabby-faced and puffy on a sort of bed. Beside her was a small table with a drink on it and around her the motionless, bright leather of the trees.

'Well, hi,' said the woman after a while and lifted a plump, bottle-shaped arm in greeting. The effort was too much for it and it flopped back on to the grass which its fingers began to stroke and pluck. The glen was a private garden at the end of the beach, set back. There seemed to be a shadowy house beyond.

'Hi,' said the blotched woman watching Mrs Filling, and Mrs Filling, blinking, said, 'Oh, I beg your pardon. Good morning. Er . . .'

'C'mon in. Press a tit.'

Mrs Filling became steel rods, then turned and began to walk quite briskly back across the beach. Astounded horror stiffened her clothes. What on earth? What on earth? And queer comfort arrived and she thought, 'But I can still be shocked. I'm only forty-eight. Some words do still shock me.'

'Hi,' called the woman on the chaise-longue, 'hi. Where you off to then? C'mon. Ring the bell. Press a tit. On the tree. C'mon back. C'mon in and have a drink, will you?' and Mrs Filling stopped because when she was not looking at her she wondered if the woman was after all so utterly disgusting.

'On the tree,' said the woman, 'look. Press it. The boy'll come.'

Nailed on to the palm tree near the woman, about five feet from the ground, was an electric bell set in a piece of wood. A wire curled up its silver stalk and then crossed the air in the direction of the shadowy house in the distance. 'That's right,' said the woman, 'press the bell. Press a tit. I never did see a gel more needin' a drink.'

Mrs Filling pressed the bell on the tree which had BOY written beneath it on the wood. She sat down on a white beach chair nearby and dabbed under her nose with her little handkerchief made into a pad. Silence fell between them; not a breaking wave, not a stirring leaf. It was about twelve noon, the sun so high there were no shadows though there was shade in the damp glade and sky-blue water lilies floating on an ornamental pond had round drops standing on their petals. A blue lizard was at Mrs Filling's feet, fat as a trout and sturdy on its pointed fingers. A big red bubble came and went under its chin. Mrs Filling was past observing it.

'So very hot,' she said faintly, and after a while, 'I've been to church.'

'Slow,' said the woman. She was listening for something. She was also munching shreds of coconut and licking her fingers. 'Slow. He's bloody slow. Bringing the drinks. Ring again, will yer, gel? Where you from?' Her legs, Mrs Filling, saw, were like tree trunks, and purple.

'England,' said Mrs Filling. She pressed the bell on the tree again. It made no sound but then the sound had far to go for the house was really quite a distance off. Looking at it, behind the woman's head, at the end of the glen it appeared to be behind a pale green haze, like a gauze curtain. Like the lost boys scene in *Peter Pan*, she thought, palm-green, Treasure Island-green, the domes of the house brass-green through the arcs of the palms and even taller trees in the greener haze behind—a poui, a cottonwood. As she looked she thought she saw the shadow of the servant leaning on a balcony, not moving.

'Can you see if he's comin', gel?'

'I—I think I can see someone.'

'Bloody nigger. Chinese, gel. Chinese. Jamaica-born Chinese nigger. Where you from?'

'England,' said Mrs Filling again. 'From Barnes, actually.' Sitting down again on the edge of the chair she felt her body wet under her nylon dress. She dabbed again at her face. 'My husband is on business here. In Kingston, that is. We are here on the North Shore just for a few days. We really wanted Montego Bay, but . . .'

'I'm Babe Jude,' said the woman. 'Jamaica-born. He's bloody Chinese nigger, hot as hell, but—God now, where he gone? You want a drink, I want a drink. See here, you go over there and get that whisky, gel—over on that table, gel. He's slow, that bloody Chink.'

Walking over for the whisky Mrs Filling was aware that she had never in her life been in conversation with anyone so dreadful and was at once in Barnes. 'I met the most appalling woman on the beach,' she was saying. (Coffee. Ellen next door. The basket chair on the patio. Dahlias.) 'Really the most frightful— Yes, awful. I don't think I have ever— No, *white*, I think. You see, in Jamaica you never really know.' She heard the new knowledge in her voice already, weeks before it spoke, and saw herself in the hairdresser's off Castelnau, sitting straighter, looking modestly down. 'And where did you go for your holidays, Mrs Filling? My! Jamaica! How marvellous! I bet that was hot. It's like a film there, isn't it?' Drawing sweet jealousy.

She felt ashamed at once, remembering Matins. She picked up the whisky and walked back to the unspeakable purple woman.

'Pour yourself a drink, gel.' The voice was kind.

'Oh, well—I'm afraid I never drink whisky.'

'Goslife, gel, pour yourself a drink.'

Mrs Filling poured herself a drink, then a drink for the woman who was holding out her glass. Turning away to replace the bottle she was surprised to see that the servant was now much nearer to them, leaning against a tree not far behind the woman and watching her. He was dressed splendidly in black trousers and a waiter's coat of sugar-pink, a black tie and boiled shirt. His face was a creamy colour, his hair wavy and long over the ears, his Chinese eyes delicately turned up at the outer ends, his mouth finely cut and turned down with a regretful and almost sweet expression, a wide space between the upper lip and fastidious nose. A silver tray was in one hand, but empty and hanging at his side. He was very still, beautiful and quite certainly bad.

Turning back to the woman Mrs Filling felt her stomach give a great lurch and that it was hard to breathe.

'Blue,' said Babe Jude, 'my Boy Blue. Little Boy Blue.

Bloody nigger. Bloody nigger Chink. Every stitch on's back I give him. Every dollar he got I get him. Out of the jungle I brought him. Set him up. Livin' in a chicken shed, sleepin' on the dirt beside a pile of rotten fruit. That was him. Boy Blue. Bloody black Chink.'

Mrs. Filling said, 'Oh dear. Oh— Oh— Please!'

'He's got a Merc.,' said Babe Jude looking into her whisky. 'I give him the Merc. Din I? Look on his wrist. You ever see a watch better'n that? Diamond ring,' she said, 'platinum. Filthy yellow nigger.'

'He's— Oh dear,' Mrs Filling gasped, 'please Mrs—er— please, I think he's here.'

'Here, is he? Good.' She raised her voice. 'Where was he before then? Where was he last night? I heard the Merc. D'you hear that, Boy? I heard the Merc. come back. Three o'clock in the morning, Boy. I'm no fool. I can't walk but I'm no fool, boy. Give us a drink, gel. I'm no fool, Chink.'

Mrs Filling's mouth opened but no sound came. Behind the tree with the bell on it she felt that the servant had moved nearer still and in the intense heat and through the dampness all over her she felt cold.

Babe Jude continued. 'It's the finish now, Boy Blue. It's finished.' Her vast, dry, powdery face had begun to shake and Mrs Filling saw that she was weeping. 'You get no more off me, man. You get no more money off me for your fancy women. Nor for your fancy men.

'I'm finished wid you, Boy Blue, see,' she shouted at her empty whisky glass. 'So find a way round that you bloody, black Chinaman.'

As the glass-bottomed boat rode in from the reef towards the white beach and its curve of pale palms, Mr Filling was surprised and embarrassed to see his wife break out of them, running fast and clutching her handbag in the heat of the day.

'Good heavens, it's my wife!' he exclaimed.

The boatman said that this seemed to be so.

'Running,' said Mr Filling, 'good gracious me, running at mid-day.'

The boatman said he didn't like to see a gel running in the heat. No, man.

'She's been in the trees,' said Mr Filling, 'in that queer glen place. Whatever has she been doing in there? I thought she'd gone to church.'

The boatman said he didn't like to see anybody going in that place. Girl or man. No. Girl or man, he said, would be better in church than that place.

'My wife is a great one for church,' said Mr Filling.

'She need every church of heaven that place,' said the boatman.

'Dear me,' said Mr Filling in a jaunty voice, considering the amount of the tip, considering his wife, still running. She had reached the jetty now. Her church hat was ridiculously crooked over one eye. She still clutched her handbag. He could see her face now, sharp and red and not beautiful. He foresaw an agitated lunch and felt depressed. Most men on business in Jamaica wisely came alone.

'You keep that gel away from that place, man,' said the boatman tossing the anchor gracefully, slowly, into the clear green sea. 'You take care of her, man. There been bad murder that place, long time back.'

2 *Missus Moon*

'I saw a funeral,' said Ned to Missus Moon.

'And how was it?' said she. She peered at her square of white crochet and big butterflies flickered round her chair and the flowering bush behind. Her chair was expensive with chromium-plated wheels. It stood by the orange bush outside the little white house where Missus Moon and her nurse lived, in the grounds of the beautiful hotel just outside Kingston. Ned was eight and loved Missus Moon who would be a hundred years old shortly.

'A shame and scandal,' said Ned.

'Is that so?'

'Shame *and* scandal,' he added. He wandered off and found a big red flower like a claw on a tree near the swimming pool and came back to lay it on her knee.

'Well now, come and see this,' said Missus Moon. 'Come here,' she called and the nurse came running. 'See what this boy has brought me today. Now see this. Take it indoors now and put it in a cup. Not in water now. You know.'

'Yes, I know, Missus Moon.'

'This is a kind boy. I have seen him before.'

'You've seen me every day,' said Ned. 'You saw me this morning.'

'Is that so?' said Missus Moon. 'And how are you today, boy?'

'I'm all right. Are you all right?'

'I'm just holdin' on,' said Missus Moon.

Ned walked in a circle round Missus Moon, touching her wheels while the nurse was in the little house putting the red claw in a cup.

'Shame and scandal,' he said in a Jamaican voice, 'sheme end scendel, ma'am, dat funeral.'

They had been on a day's outing to Ocho Rios when there had suddenly been great crowds all over the road. People in white hats and half a hundred vicars. Choirs. Church ladies and crowds of blue-black men in blue-black suits. Buses. One bus was called Treasure Girl in curly letters and another Happy Jo. A truck was stuck and cars all tilting anyhow along the side of the fields. Everyone had excited faces and was very tidy and smily. Their car—Daddy and Mummy and Ned's—was nearly tipped up by a bus. The bus ground against their wing and out got about a thousand vicars all in purple and scarlet, all talking and smiling. They were tightly squeezed—Mummy and Daddy and Ned—between the bus and a glass-sided taxi with a shiny box in it with golden handles.

'What's that?' Ned had asked and Mummy had said, 'Oh Ned, do look at the pretty children. Look at their pretty white dresses.' Ned had looked behind however out of the car window and seen the flood of lacy vicars and crowds and crowds all gathering in a sort of dell in a scrubby meadow. There had been a cross held up in the air and everyone talking and waiting to start. The back of the big taxi was down in a flap and a hot man in a stiff collar was bellowing about and crying, 'Where are the bearers? Oh Lord! Pass by man, pass by! Oh, shame and scandal, where are the bearers?'

'What's bearers?' Ned had asked.

'Oh that's better,' said his mother. 'Look, dear, they've freed the big truck. We'll be off in a minute.'

A wave of song broke from the scruffy glade, which had a dip in it and fresh earth and everyone jolly and talking round it. But the hot man still asked God to send the bearers and an important fat lady in a lot of black net went by with a big white handkerchief against her mouth and her eyes above it looking around excitedly.

'Shame and scandal.'

'What is it, Mummy? What is it, Daddy?'

'A funeral.'

'That funeral,' he said now, circling back to Missus Moon and putting on her knee another flower, yellow this time, 'were a shame and scandal. A sheme and a scendel.'

'You talking Jamaican, boy,' said Missus Moon, 'now where's my girl? Tell her I don't seem to be able to round this corner.'

'What you knitting?'

'A baby blanket,' said Missus Moon. 'Now where's my girl gone? Now I'm making it all the time, boy. You see me making it every day you visit me. I am tired now, boy. You go off now and let me be quiet.'

He went off and stood under the bean tree and saw the nurse, square and black and beautiful in her white wings, come back to Missus Moon without the red claw and carrying a cup of milk. 'Now here's your milk, Missus Moon.'

'You're not to leave me you know,' said Missus Moon, 'you're not to leave me for a minute. Those are your instructions, girl. Who is that boy under the bean tree?'

'Why, he's Ned, Missus Moon. He gave you a flower.'

'Good. Tell him he may come and talk to me some time. Tomorrow when I am round the corner of this blanket. And who is this coming now?'

It was Ned's mother looking for Ned and wanting to be introduced to Missus Moon who as everybody had heard would soon be a hundred years old and was immensely rich and recently widowed. Mr Moon had been ninety-seven. They had lived in the hotel for thirty years. Missus Moon sat apart in her shining wheel-chair in exactly the same place each day, under the orange bush with her square of white crochet, her coffee-cream arms like sticks under a loose, white cotton dress. She shone on the grass. All the guests, even the Bolivians, became unaware of themselves for a moment as they passed her by.

'Excuse me,' said Ned's mother in a tolerant, pleasant voice, aiming to please, 'I believe my son— I hope he doesn't tire you?'

'Who is this coming now?' said Missus Moon to the nurse. 'How do you do?' You could see her glance had once been sharp.

'How do you do?' said Ned's mother gently.

'Thank you, dear. I'm just holdin' on.'

'Ha ha ha,' laughed Ned's mother and smiling wondered what to say next. She saw Ned under the bean tree pointing an imaginary gun at Missus Moon and at her. He made a noise of a machine-gun and then the scream of falling bombs. 'Hush,' she cried, 'you will upset Missus Moon.'

'He's been to a funeral,' said Missus Moon. 'Let him continue. Now I wonder how he came to be at a funeral.'

'Oh,' Ned's mother blushed and looked away from Missus Moon's hands which were stained with brown patches and ridged like chicken's feet. 'Oh dear. He tells such tales. Please don't let him tire you. That is really what I came to say.'

'He is my friend,' said Missus Moon. 'Now you must go because I am just about to turn this corner.' Ned's mother, feeling set down, went self-consciously away to the pool, calling Ned to come and practise his crawl. To come *at once*.

'Did you go to your father's funeral?' asked Ned.

Missus Moon put her crochet square on her lap and looked quizzically over Ned's head at the great black pods hooked all over the bean tree. He came closer.

'Has your father just had a funeral?' The nurse was in the little house, warming the milk. It was next day.

'Come here, boy,' said Missus Moon. 'Come and look at this baby blanket.'

'You haven't done much more,' he said. 'It never grows much. It'll have to be a small baby.'

'It'll have to be a very small baby, boy,' said Missus Moon. They both laughed, Ned loudly. He hung over the arm of her chair.

'Have you good eyes?' he asked.

'I have no eyes,' she said, 'look at my eyes. I have no sight in one of my eyes.'

'Which?' asked Ned, looking closely. He leaned over and felt her eye lids.

'I forget,' said Missus Moon and again they both laughed.

'That one looks the worst,' he said. 'Does it hurt?'

'Not at all. Not at all, boy.'

'Did your father have bad eyes?'

Missus Moon looked abstracted. 'Father?' she said.

'Who just had a funeral.'

'But it was you went to the funeral.'

Ned looked closely at her face. 'Are you black or white?' he said.

'That I can't say,' said Missus Moon. 'It is not of consequence.'

'How do you do?' she called to a fat little Cuban with

a soft face and sloping shoulders. He bowed. 'What rounded trousers,' she said. A lady came by, a little busi-ness-man's wife from Barnes, shy, trying out Bermuda shorts. In earrings. 'Ah, how do you do? Yes, thank you. I'm holdin' on dear.'

'Did you go to Missus Moon's father's funeral?' Ned asked the nurse who gave a cry and a start that set the milk cup rattling. 'Father? Away you go now,' she said, 'Missus Moon must rest now. Dear Lord have mercy on us all!

'It was her *husband*. Three months past,' she whispered, leading Ned away. 'Now don't upset her. She has quite forgotten.'

Next day Missus Moon was not outside her bungalow. Ned hung about. Her shutters were down and the howling noise of the air conditioning machine could be heard within. The nurse was inside too, and the doctor, and there was talking and a good deal of coming and going. Ned picked a lot of flowers and great, black rattling bean pods and arranged them on the ground outside the bunga-low in patterns. At length the nurse came out looking agitated.

'Where's Missus Moon?' he asked.

'Now you go off and swim in the pool,' said the nurse. 'Are you going off to the beach today now?'

'I want to see Missus Moon.'

'I want to see Missus Moon,' he said at lunch in the hotel restaurant.

'I believe she's not well, dear.'

'Will she die?'

'Eat your fruit.'

'I want to see Missus Moon *now*,' said Ned.

'You are going to sleep now,' said his mother, gathering his wrist into a firm grip and smiling at everyone in a very easy way as she went out, holding him fast, a little on her left flank.

As they passed Missus Moon's bungalow on their way in to dinner that evening the lights were on but there was no sound. 'I might just call in,' he said, but was ignored.

He said no more. The next day he and his parents went to the North Shore for a long stay. They were to come back to the lovely hotel with the bungalows just for a night at the very end, on the way to catch the aeroplane home. At the North Shore he forgot all about Missus Moon and concentrated instead on a lizard that showed off to him night and day, doing press-ups on his balcony, and on the frogs that held on to the edges of the lily pond with little hands, like beginners at swimming lessons. There were sea urchins in the sea and striped blue and yellow fish and tree frogs and vultures and a humming bird with a curly tail. Someone helped him make a sand-castle on the beach. There were crab races and a fire-eater and a steel band. He played the drums in the band one night because Jamaicans are so kind to children, and all the Americans came up on their haunches to take photographs of him with cameras that looked like ray guns.

The night before they left he grew very wild and sprang about the bedroom. Then he sprang about the terraces and knocked over somebody's dry martini and tried to trip up a beautiful lady in a long dress. Finally he lay down on the dance floor and kicked and carried on and said he wasn't going to bed.

'You have behaved scandalously,' said his father, 'and I am ashamed.' Ned wept but he fell asleep at last, hot and violent and in dudgeon. Not himself.

On the road back, beyond Ocho Rios, the next day they passed the scruffy hollow where the taxi with the flap had been and the lorry had got stuck, but there were no people there now. Ned set up a great singing.

'Well now,' his mother said brightly as they reached the beautiful hotel in the south again. 'Only one more night left. Look dear, there is Missus Moon.' Under the orange bush was the shiny chair, the white square of crochet and Missus Moon holding it. It was rather bigger.

'Are you better, Missus Moon?' Ned's mother's voice sounded more confident.

'I am better, dear,' Missus Moon replied, 'I am holdin' on. Now who is this? And who is this boy?'

'I'm Ned,' said Ned, 'I'm your friend.' He swung tremendously on her chair arm. 'Your eye looks better a bit. Don't you remember me? I've been away.'

'And so have I,' said Missus Moon. She looked at him closely. After a while she said, 'Have you been to any more funerals?'

'No,' he said.

'Shame and scandal,' she quoted laughing.

'Sheme end scendel,' said Ned.

'You talk Jamaican, boy.' They laughed together. 'Now, will you be staying long?'

'No,' he said, 'I have to go.'

'Dear me,' said she.

'We have to go home. It's school.'

'Now that's a shame,' said Missus Moon, 'for I intend remainin'.'

The best day of my Easter holidays was the day we met
Jolly Jackson. This year we went to Jamaica for our
holidays because my father was working there and so we
spent all his fees although it was still expensive and we
didn't get any rake-off. When I told all the American
people in our hotel we were there on my father's fees they
thought it was very funny and said things to my father
like 'I hear you're travelling light, bud,' and slapped him
over the back in a way that puzzled him and made him
angry.

The people in our hotel were all very, very rich. One
was so rich he got paralysed, the beach boy told me. Like
Midas one side of him got turned to gold. He dribbled.
The only one not rich was a vicar. He had gone there to
a conference. My mother met him in the sea and they
talked up to their knees. 'How lucky we are,' said the vicar
in a HUGE American accent, 'in this so glorious country,
enjoying the gifts of God. It is Eden itself.' Then he
shouted 'FLAMING HADES' and fell flat on his stomach in
the sea because he had been stung by a sea-egg. 'Help,
help,' called my mother and everyone came running off
the beach and dragged the vicar up the sand—blood everywhere. 'Ammonia!' cried someone. 'Only thing for a sea-
egg is to pee on it,' said the beach-raker. 'Git gone,' said
the beach-boy and my mother said, 'Come along now Ned
dear, it's time we set off for Duns River Falls.' The other

women turned away, too and only the men were left standing around the vicar who had five black spikes sticking out of his foot and was rolling about in agony. 'They never do no permanent harm, ma'am,' said the beach-boy to my mother, 'just pain and anguish for a day,' and he was laughing like anything—well, like a Jamaican and they laugh a great deal. I don't know if they did try peeing on the vicar or if they did if it was one or all of them. I kept thinking of the whole crowd standing round and peeing on the vicar and I laughed like a Jamaican all the way to Duns River Falls until my parents said, 'Shut up or there'll be trouble.'

Duns River Falls are some waterfalls that drop into the sea. I had expected them about as high as a tower but they were only about as high as my father. Also they had built a road over them and kiosks etc., and ticket offices and I was fed up because I had wanted to stay on the beach.

My mother said, 'Well, now we're here—' and we began to park the car when a huge man came dancing along the road in pink and blue clothes and a straw hat and opened the door and shook hands with my father. 'Hullo Daddy,' he shouted, 'an' how are you today?' (Everyone starts 'An' how are you today.') 'Now then Daddy, outs you get and in the back. I gonna sit with Mummy.'

Now my father is a man who is very important at home and nobody tells him what to do. In Jamaica he doesn't wear his black suit and stiff collar or his gold half-glasses, but even in an orange shirt and a straw hat you can tell he is very important. Oh yes man. But when this great big man told him to get out and sit in the back he got out and sat in the back, and my mother's eyes went large and wide. 'Stop for nobody and dat's advice,' they had said in our hotel, 'Jamaica is a very inflammatory place. Yes sir.'

Well this man held out the biggest hand I've ever seen, pink on the front, and said, 'My name's Jolly Jackson and what's yours?'

My father said, 'Hum. Hum. Ahem,' but my mother said, 'Mrs Egerton,' and held out her hand and I sprang up and down and said, 'My name's Ned, man,' and my father said, 'That will do.'

'This boy talks Jamaican, yes sir,' said Jolly Jackson, 'and now I gonna take you to see the wonderful Public Gardens followed by a tour of the surrounding countryside where you will find growing, pineapples, coffee beans, tea, avocado, coconuts and every single thing. Every fruit in all the world grow in Jamaica. Jamaica is the best country in the world and the sun is always shining.'

At that moment it began to rain in the most tremendous torrents and as our car was going up a hill which was probably once part of the waterfall and going about the same sort of angle, great waves began to come rushing down on us and the car spluttered and stopped and then turned sideways and began to be washed away.

'This is one of the famous Jamaican rainstorms,' said Jolly Jackson. 'The rain in Jamaica is the best in the world. It is very necessary rain. It rushes over the ground and disappears into the sea. In a minute it will be gone.'

We sat there for about half an hour and the rain hit the road like ten million bullets and went up from it in steam and the trees above dripped it back. Waves washed round our sideways wheels and my mother said, 'What happens if a car comes the other way?'

'Don't worry,' said Jolly Jackson, 'everything stop in a Jamaica rainstorm,' and then a huge great petrol tanker with all its lights on came tearing round the corner and down the hill towards us, screeched its brakes and skidded into the side of the road and fell into a ditch.

'Here comes the sun now,' said Jolly Jackson in a hasty voice, 'away we go,' and he got the car going and turned up the hill again and off before the driver of the petrol tanker had got the door open and got a look at us.

He was right and the sun came out and everything shone and steamed. When we got to the Public Gardens Jolly Jackson put his foot on the accelerator and roared through, past the ticket office. He was out and had all of us out in about a quarter of a second and all of us off down a path before my mother could even mop up her face.

'This here is the famous Jamaica red tree,' he said. 'This here is oleander, that there is the ban-yan tree only fifty year old, big as a mountain. That there is a waterfall. Now this boy and Mummy are gonna stand in the water-fall and have a photo.' He took the camera from round my father's neck, undid it and went click, click. Sometimes he turned the camera towards himself and went click, click and my father said, 'I say, look here—'

'Now,' he said, 'you will take a photograph of me,' and he stood inside a very dark trellis tunnel full of great big pale green lilies like long bells hanging, and stretched up and smelled one, arching his very long back, and a big white smile on his face. He stood there for a very long time even though my mother said 'It's in the dark.' In the end she said, 'Oh well,' and went click and then Jolly Jackson moved on.

I've never seen my parents go so fast. He simply ran up and down paths, in and out of groves and places, pointing things out, picking things—sometimes great huge branches of things. 'Take it, take it. Plenty more. Jamaica can grow everything.' Once he stopped dead and we all crashed into his back. He gathered us all together and said, 'Look now, just there. That is the true Jamaica humming bird,' and there of course was a humming bird with its lovely curly tail. It was sipping from a rosy flower. There are thousands of them at our hotel all round our table at lunch every single day. We didn't even notice them much after the first week, but now we all said 'Ooooooooooh.' Jolly Jackson somehow made you say 'Ooooooooooh.' Yes man.

Well, before my mother had seen half she wanted to he shovelled us into the car again and we stormed the barricades like James Bond or something and were off up a terribly narrow stony road with little Jamaican chicken-hut houses on each side in the trees and ladies doing their washing with lovely pink and yellow handkerchiefs on their heads, but we went so fast we couldn't get more than glimpses. My father said, leaning forward and tapping Jolly Jackson's shoulder, 'I think I should just mention that the car is only insured for myself,' and Jolly Jackson said, 'Now don't you worry Daddy, I been driving ten years. I fully qualified Private Guide and never an accident yet.' Just then a police car came rocketing round the corner and got into a tangle with our front bumper which fell off. 'Never mind,' said Jolly Jackson, 'these are my friends,' and everybody got out. There were three police men and two police women and they all laughed and laughed and shook hands with Jolly Jackson and Jolly Jackson introduced us. 'This is Daddy,' he said. 'A very important man in business from London, England, this is Ned and this is Mummy who is just at home.' This annoyed my mother who does a lot of writing work at home and gives speeches on how women are as important as men.

Well, we picked up the bumper and Jolly Jackson tried to put it in the boot and then threw it away under a banana tree. Then we went to see a lot of his aunts, cousins, great aunts, grandmothers and mother. They were all very nice and gathered round the car and told us about all their daughters who were all matrons in hospitals in London. Jolly Jackson's mother said that his sister was matron of several hospitals in London. 'That right,' said Jolly Jackson, 'my sister called Polly Jackson. I Jolly Jackson. She Polly Jackson. You go back to London and ask for Polly Jackson. She'll be there.'

My mother said to my father, 'I don't believe all this is happening.'

At one chicken-house place a whole lot of children gathered round who all seemed to be relations. One of them put his tongue out at me and said 'White face', but Jolly Jackson hit him. My father, after we'd waited simply ages gave some dollars round and we went on. Once we went up a very steep road and stopped to see coffee growing by the road and a woman came out of the trees, very pretty, with a baby with a sore leg. The leg had gone yellow, orange and purple all round the cut. She had cut it on a bottle last week, the mother said. The baby was hot and crying and my mother said, 'That child has a temperature, he needs penicillin,' (very fierce) and the mother of the baby drew back with a cold look and said, 'No Missis, I put on coconut oil. You think me Jamaican monkey.' A bad look passed between them. The woman said 'white face' and my father said, 'Oh come now' and handed more dollars.

'Do you think things are going to change in Jamaica?' my father asked Jolly Jackson as we went tearing on after this and he said, still in the same happy voice, 'Oh yes, man. Ninety thousand soldiers.' Actually he might have said, 'Nine thousand soldiers,' or 'Nineteen thousand soldiers' but it sounded like 'Ninety thousand soldiers,' and after that we were all quiet for a bit.

We seemed somehow after a very long time to get back to the same place, I don't know how. But it was terribly hot in the car and we didn't have any idea where we were. Then we saw the petrol tanker in the ditch and crowds and crowds trying to get it out and everybody smiling. Jolly Jackson's police friends were there and a lot of his other friends and we all got out again to shake hands, and we bought a pineapple for one dollar thirty which made my mother say, 'Fortnum and Mason!' Jolly Jackson introduced us to hundreds of his friends. Afterwards we went back towards the Falls again and we nearly hit another car and the driver leaned out and shouted a lot of queer language at us ending in Jackson. 'Is he your friend, too?' my mother asked, and Jolly Jackson said, 'No, I know him but he is not my friend.'

'Now, we all go in the Falls,' he said when we got to the parking place. 'All take off your clothes and we walk up the Falls, five hundred feet of pure Jamaican waterfall. Perfectly safe. Nobody never falls in, never.'

'NO,' said my father and gave him six dollars.

'Seven,' said Jolly Jackson, and my father gave him seven dollars, and we went off to look at the Falls by ourselves, my mother saying things like, 'Quite ridiculous. You are an utter fool, James. Daylight robbery,' and my father saying it was worth it just to be still alive.

Somehow going up the Falls was very dull though, without Jolly Jackson and we didn't stay long. Everyone looked very white and ugly and touristy and quiet. My mother even said as we left, and went to the car again, 'I suppose seven dollars was *enough*, James? He really did us rather well I suppose. We did *see* a lot. It took two hours.' But my father said 'Pah! Enough! Look!' and we saw Jolly Jackson by the car park all alone and dancing in the road.

I said I wanted to go and say goodbye to him again but they said, no. I said it wouldn't take long but they said, no dear, come along. 'Come along,' they said. 'Let's go back to the beach, let's see what's happened to the poor old vicar.' But that—the silly vicar and the man all paralysed with gold—didn't interest me any more. All that interested me was Jolly Jackson and I watched him and watched him, so beautiful, out of the back window of the car, getting smaller and smaller. And he waved and waved to me as he danced and danced. He danced and danced not moving his feet but with all his body and his lovely smiling face. He was dancing and dancing and dancing and dancing in the very middle of the big main road.

That was the best day of my Easter holidays.

(B—Egerton. Rubbish. See me.)

4   *The Pool Boy*

For years in her quiet way and particularly in Harrods
Lady Fletcher (wife of the judge) had looked forward to the
title. She received it and was disappointed.

It was not that in Harrods the most surprising people
have titles now. It was not that her daily help who had
wandering thoughts didn't cotton on, or that the dry-
cleaner who called on Tuesdays and the laundry (Thurs-
days) had known her for years as Fletcher Number 22 and
would not change now. It was not that her friends called
her Enid as before, just rather louder 'You know Enid
Fletcher, don't you?'—though all this was certainly rather
sad. No—it went further.

Some ancient accident long forgotten—a silly book
perhaps, or the local Lady Something when Enid had been
a child at Swanage, in the draper's, someone tall,
emaciated, with a blazing blue stare and rings that might
have told a tale—something like this may have stirred in
the square, solid little girl an envy and a conviction that
a title meant romance. A mistake.

Lord Fletcher, a quiet man keen on bird-watching, was
quite unaware of his wife's disappointment. There were
those who said he was quite unaware of his wife, though
this was unjust for he had shown himself to be perfectly
satisfied with her at all times and particularly satisfied by
her utterly reliable behaviour in their dark, bow-fronted
Wimbledon house facing the Common—the dustless order,

the excellent dinners always on time. Oxtail on Fridays. Asked on the Bench, as he was very occasionally, about his wife's diversions (they were childless), he said she had a finger in various good works and was very fond of cooking.

And so she had and so she was. And she liked the order of her life. She had not been at all unhappy their twenty-four years of evenings together in the fawn and cream sitting-room, Lewis under the standard lamp, the eternal arc of papers spread about his feet, the bright pink blobs of tape on the fat arm of the easy chair. 'The original red tape,' he called it.

She liked her occasional luncheons given to other Wimbledon ladies and legal wives—never more than four —round the big mahogany table, the silver properly polished and through the window of the tidy shorn garden with the well-pruned hybrid teas, the pampas clump— though she did occasionally wish that she saw her friends more often and that it was not sometimes a year or more before anyone invited anyone else back.

She went on the Common every day with the dog and after years, when the dog was dead, she still walked there each afternoon watching picnics and tramps and the sinful cars drawn up under the trees and clusters of horses going by with proud-faced riders and the little girls from the school in the Crescent playing rounders, all their cardigans in a soft heap by the games mistress, who watched them play and now and then called out, 'Oh *nicely*, Susan,' clapping her hands.

She liked the way the electric fire was switched on always half an hour before dinner and switched off again by Lewis as they left the dining-room each evening, year in, year out. She liked Lewis.

But her life lacked occurrences and mistakenly and she

A2

realised now, ridiculously, she had expected the title to bring them.

'Lewis,' she had said, 'congratulations.'

'Congratulations,' he had said and kissed her. 'Congratulations, Lady Fletcher.'

'Oh really, Lewis! I don't suppose I shall take it up.'

They had dined with champagne at Rule's that evening —early though already Rule's was rather dark. They were almost alone there. She had worn a new dress, from Marshall and Snelgrove—expensive and ageing (she had rather a sloping chest) and afterwards they had had to go straight home again as the judge had papers.

At least, Lady Fletcher thought, Christmas will be better now. At Christmas was the Chambers sherry party where for years—as Mrs Fletcher—she had felt herself increasingly out of touch, her hair too tidy, her jewellery too quiet and good, her conversation trailing off into the nods and smiles of a ninny among the younger and younger wives who were all so clever and competent (one played the French horn), some of them with professions themselves. This year, however, with the ripeness of the title, even against a French horn she would hold her own.

What had slipped her mind was that since her husband was now no longer a member of Chambers and on Circuit in December, they would not be invited.

Christmas came and went at their usual hotel at Rye which Lewis liked because of the birds on the marshes. She read the new Iris Murdoch and talked of television and recipes with other middle-aged wives. They went over to Winchelsea and walked about the ruins in cold rain. The hotel was too hot but the bath water unpredictable. On Christmas Day, paper-hatted but not talkative, at small tables, everyone ate turkey cooked on Christmas Eve. She felt shivery and took the 'flu. 'I'll have it at home,' she thought as though it were a baby, and the judge drove slowly back in the sleet to Wimbledon where the 'flu became a long and painful attack of bronchitis.

'You need the sun,' said the doctor, 'the Bahamas. You don't want Wimbledon in January.'

The judge said that it was a mild winter and Wimbledon clement.

'Depressing though,' said the doctor. 'Can't you get her somewhere a bit brighter? West Indies?'

Lady Fletcher said that she would be quite all right here at home and really the Bahamas—West Indies— were surely for film stars and people like Noël Coward.

'Noël Coward's what you need,' said the doctor. 'Come on now, Lady Fletcher. We'll make a film star of you yet.

'I'd really advise it,' he said to the judge at the door, and the judge stood in the hall among the Edwardian panels for quite some time after he had gone, thinking. He was capable of thought and even of decision, being unusual in his profession. Lady Fletcher was in Jamaica in a week, though in all the wrong clothes.

In the thinnest of these she lay by the pool of the beautiful hotel outside Kingston under a yellow cotton tree. The guests mostly lived in white bungalows about the grounds and between these bungalows in the gold sunshine the square black maids walked in dresses of pink and white cotton, their fat faces always smiling and shining, their dark, round hands lifted twenty times a day in a wave.

'An' how are you to*day*, Lady Fletcher, ma'am?'

'I'm *very* well, Lavinia.'

'Oh, that's very good now, my lady, ma'am.'

Waiters in banana-yellow coats appeared silently with trays of rum and orange juice.

'My, you lookin' better today, Lady Fletcher, my lady. You got a light in the eye, ma'am.'

'I don't know about the eye,' she said, delighted. 'I do feel very well.'

'You goin' to be stayin' with us now two, three months, my lady?'

'Oh dear—I hope so. But I'm afraid not.'

At the end of a week, in a new apple-green cotton dress and white sandals and a shampoo and set from a most relaxing hairdresser (the clients seemed to stay all day considering various unweighty matters, and all the chairs had little heaps of wool surrounding them on the floor), her skin a golden pink, Enid Fletcher lay serene.

She lay—always by the pool—imagining, as the days went on and she grew golder and pinker yet, Good Friday, when Lewis would arrive. Sometimes in the sleepy sunshine she almost saw him in fact, dark-suited, sharp-faced, hot, coming off the plane, over the stones round the pool's edge to meet her. But weeks, weeks away—stooping to kiss her cheek.

'Very good-looking.'

'What, dear?'

'I said, "You're a very good-looking woman."'

The languid movement of her arm towards her glass, her confident upward smile. 'Dear Lewis. You look hot.' None of the silent wonder she would have felt at such a statement at home. Acceptance and friendly ease.

Because there by the pool from the very beginning Enid Fletcher had found her kingdom and in it had held her court. Everyone came to the pool, at least once a day. Pad, pad, pad they came, at eight and one and five o'clock. 'Good morning', 'Good afternoon', 'Good evening,

Lady Fletcher, lovely day.' Splash. After a swim they pressed a bell for drinks, beat themselves about the shoulders and thighs with towels, then settled beside her on the smooth stones or on the long chairs, oiling themselves, the men wriggling strong, brown toes.

Mr Luft was the first. An American, dark, copper-coloured, huge. Immensely handsome. Not too young either—at least forty-five and covered all over in curly dark hair like Tarzan. He had Tarzan-like teeth, too, and dark crimson swimming trunks (narrow) and the most splendid gold watch with a gold-ribbed strap which glinted under the water in the sun.

'Oh— You've forgotten your watch,' she cried the first time she saw him, swimming strongly towards her through the green water, before they had even been introduced—on her very first day.

'That's O.K.,' he said, heaving himself out on bulging muscles, 'waterproof.'

'Oh, but they never really are!'

'This one is, Ma'am. It's a real stinger. What you drinking? Name's Luft. Hal Luft.'

'I'm—er—Enid Fletcher.'

'Hi then, Enid. What you drinking?'

There began a pleasant and, since Luft was always the very earliest home from the business of the day in Kingston, a very private conversation, private save only for the pool boy who hardly ever lifted his eyes.

Next, after his rest, came the child Ned, and his rather over-smiling mother, then a Mrs Filling, a jumpy lady feeling the heat, rather skinless about the nose. 'A menopause lady,' thought Lady Fletcher, then remembered that she herself was fifty. There were the handsome South Americans who only spoke Spanish but who smiled and bowed a great deal, a dazzling Bolivian beauty with a gracious acknowledgement of the head. And there was Mr McCrindle.

'It's an interesting name, McCrindle,' said Lady Fletcher. 'Is it Scottish?'

'That I cannot say,' said Mr McCrindle, 'for I am a Cuban.'

'A Cuban! How exciting! But I thought—'

'Ah,' he said softly—he was a very little man and blond, with a small, English, military moustache and sloping shoulders like a debutante, 'I'm a B.C. Cuban.'

'Goodness!'

'A B.C. Cuban is a Before Castro Cuban. I am an exile, ma'am. I travel between the Latin-American offices of my Canadian and American companies as far apart as the Pacific Ocean, Lima in Peru and Panama, and here, in the West Indies. I have of course firmly established a domicile for myself in the southern part of the United States. I fly constantly. Last night I flew in from Cuzco and there, ma'am, I would advise you—but I expect you know Cuzco already?'

Lady Fletcher said, 'No.'

'I advise you to plan no activity for twelve hours after your aeroplane has landed there. You will find that any kind of exertion is impossible. You will even wake from sleep to find that you are almost unable to move on account of the altitude and the lowered speed of the circulation of the blood. Fortunately there are always oxygen appliances placed at each bedside. The height of the hotel is twelve thousand feet. I resort very frequently to whiffs in the night.'

'How very alarming!' (How far from Rye!)

'But I advise you, Lady Fletcher, whenever you are in South America, not to miss a flight over Lake Titicaca. I flew over it myself not twelve hours since and I was once again moved almost to tears by the curious beauty of the surface and the fact that the shores are often not visible. One might in fact be flying over a great ocean. It is—as of course you know—the highest inland sea in the whole world. You must be sure to go there. Though of course you must know it already?'

His voice, light, passionless, clear, flowed restfully on imparting information in carefully extended sentences. They poured effortlessly out from under his pale moustache like ectoplasm, she thought; like Athene emerging from the head of Zeus.

Then, 'Whatever made me think that?' she asked herself. She felt delighted once again. Her head, caressed by the sun and peace was casting up all kinds of treasures she had thought quite lost.

Sometimes during the day of course, when the men were at their business deals and the sight-seers sight-seeing, she was quite alone by the pool—alone except for the pool boy whose job it was, all day long, to walk round its edge with a long shrimping net casting for spiders, wasps and leaves. Sometimes he slowly swept the leaves together that had gathered on the paving stones about the pool. He caught them slowly into a pile with his long flippy brush, and regarded them for a time before putting them in a basket. He was a big, thick young man, taller even than Hal Luft, his legs alone almost as tall as the whole of Mr McCrindle. He wore khaki shorts or sometimes workman's denim trousers. His skin was the colour of grapes and he walked with a gentle, sleepy step on bare blue feet, his face thoughtful and apart. He was utterly silent. Lady Fletcher came to think of him as one of the trees or plants about her, nearer to the bean pods or the lizards or the birds or the sun than to Luft or McCrindle or the rest. Sometimes she fell asleep in her long chair and awoke to find herself still alone an hour later with the pool boy still casting his net gently into the same part of the water. She said good morning to him of course each day and he moved his head in what was perhaps a bow. Otherwise he acknowledged her no more than if she had been the air about them.

One evening after five Luft came back to the hotel after work rather later than usual. It was very hot—hot as June, Lavinia said. He called, 'Hi,' and flung himself and his gold watch into the pool, swam across, heaved himself out, sat down beside her and put a hand upon her thigh.

Before she could quite think, McCrindle appeared through the hibiscus bushes, also in bathing trunks and carrying a snorkel which he was trying ridiculously to fit over his small head as he walked. On his feet were big black flippers. He was already beginning one of his sentences.

He stopped at the pool's edge. Luft at once removed his hand. 'Hi, Mac,' he called, 'c'mon and join the party.' McCrindle turned and disappeared.

That evening Lewis arrived from England—pale but quite jaunty—and they dined in the hotel. Neither Luft nor McCrindle was present. That night, later, when she sat with the judge and some Jamaican lawyers and friends on the terrace, McCrindle came hurriedly through the bar and cut Lady Fletcher dead.

She felt wretched, almost tearful, and another new and at first unrecognised emotion not altogether disagreeable. She talked pleasantly and more than usual. The dazzling Bolivian woman who had joined the party asked the judge if he did not think his wife looked well. He said, looking at her quickly and then away, 'Very,' and she knew what it was she felt. She felt powerful.

For the time of the year it was a very hot night. When the friends had gone the reunited Fletchers stood on the wide wooden balcony of the hotel for a time, looking at the stars and the clusters of lights so high in the mountains they might also have been stars. They walked in the grounds a little and hoped it would be cool in the new room they were to share that night. Lady Fletcher had slept in the hotel until now and had not been in one of the garden bungalows while on her own.

'It's the bungalow by the pool, dear,' she said, 'Lavinia moved our things in and unpacked for us both during dinner. It seems a waste when we are going off tomorrow to the north, but it will be nicer there. You will be able to get straight out of bed and swim before breakfast.'

'I hope it won't be noisy,' said the judge. 'Do they sit out round there at night?'

'Oh, I'm sure not,' she said, 'there are no lights. And all the children will be in bed.'

'Let's hope so. I'm tired. Eleven hours' flying. It's six hours onwards for me, you know. It's five in the morning already for me now.'

'Does it seem madness?' she asked. She put her arm through his. 'To have come?'

He said, 'No, not madness,' and was soon asleep.

But Lady Fletcher was restless. She was not at all sure that she liked the new room as well as the other which had been up on the first floor of the hotel and behind a regal balcony, high above the scufflings in the grass. This bed seemed harder, she didn't like having to keep the shutters up. ('You lock yourselves in that bungalow now, Lady Fletcher,' Lavinia had said, 'these times is inflammatory.') And she kept on hearing footsteps around the pool behind them. Once she switched on the bedside lamp and

B

was eye to eye with a very long lizard on the bedside telephone. To try to get to sleep she began to allow herself uncharacteristic thoughts and fancies. They expanded into scenes, almost stories that insisted on the presence of new friends, particularly of Hal Luft and Mr McCrindle. She dozed at last and dreamed of being caught in nets.

Then she was quite awake and sitting up in bed, her eyes wide open and round. Outside, behind the bed, so close it seemed to be almost in her ear, she heard a light, passionless, almost plaintive voice. Although it was so close she could not distinguish words but the cadences, the pauses, the insistence, the eternal, practised flow were unmistakable. McCrindle must be sitting by the pool, just behind her up the steps, behind her through the wall, the sound coming through the louvres of the little garden door. He must be sitting by the pool and talking to himself.

Lying down again and listening to Lewis's heavy breathing, Lady Fletcher shut her eyes and heard the voice flow on and on. It was so near, so intimate, that she felt (how hot it was! She flung off the sheet) she felt that he— McCrindle—was almost there with her. She shivered, for her earlier fancies had not gone in any way so far. She found herself shocked and blushing.

On and on went the voice and, as she listened, it dawned on her—she did not know how—that Mr McCrindle was not alone. He was with one other person. One other person. One who was keeping silent. The two people must be together by the pool. And somehow she knew that whoever they were, whoever was with him was —well, not standing up or moving about. Never before would she have imagined that you can tell from a voice whether or not it comes from an upright position. Beyond doubt this voice reclined.

Yet it was urgent. On and on. On and on. Minutes passed and it began again, gentler now. Less querulous. More—what? More almost seductive. There was a laugh now, and then—yes—another laugh, much deeper.

'I must,' said Lady Fletcher, 'I must see.' Silently she got out of bed and walked on bare quiet feet, forgetting lizards, Lewis, everything, and went to the little garden door in the lobby behind her bed. The first laugh came again, Mr McCrindle's light laugh.

All she could see through the fixed wooden shutter of the door was a narrow oblong slit perhaps twelve inches by two. It showed only the three cement steps leading up to the pool, the urn at their top and a length of wide chaise-longue with some legs lying on it. But it was moonlight and the moonlight caught a glitter of something beside the urn. Something. A something. A wrist. The wrist curled round someone else's neck. The wrist was covered with black hairs and was encircled by a magnificent gold watch. In the moonlight the light laugh came again, followed by the deep and unmistakable laugh of Luft. She let the shutter clatter loudly down. 'Hullo,' called Lewis. Outside there was silence.

Next morning, all alone, Lady Fletcher lay and watched the pool boy gracefully fishing. Lewis was gone to negotiate the hired car. They were to set off after lunch for the North Shore—to begin to see Jamaica. They would come back here only for the last night, just to buy their presents in Kingston—the honey, the rum, and some raffia dinner mats (the dinner mats in Wimbledon were worn out). She and Lewis would be alone together now and she would never sit here by the pool again.

Never again.

Her gaze never left the pool boy. She followed every

movement of his net, the spread of his arms, the sinews in his legs. He looked up at her at length, straight into her face and waited.

'Last night,' she said, 'the most extraordinary thing. I heard lovers talking by the pool. It must have been three o'clock in the morning.'

His face was still.

'The curious thing,' she went on with a laugh, not keeping down her voice, looking at her smart, pink nails, 'the curious thing was, I looked out and it was—well, it was two men.'

The pool boy went on staring at her for a while and not a leaf stirred. She did not look at him in case she did not see what she so much needed—or saw the derision she so feared. At length he said, turning back to the pool, 'Sometimes it is so.' He straightened up again and this time their eyes met each other. He said gently, 'Some strange things are so.'

'Well, I must pack now,' she said briskly after a moment. 'We leave today. Goodbye.' He said no more and she went sensibly into the bungalow past the urn and down the little steps, and inside the bungalow stood a long time in the middle of the room not moving.

After perhaps a very long time she realised that she had been looking at herself unseeing, in the long mirror between the windows, windows shuttered still, but now against the light. In the shadowy quiet room she stood and looked, looked and looked, focusing at last on the image of the perfect stranger in the mirror that she would never see again.

'I want him,' she said to it, 'I want him.'

The face of the stranger began to blush and tears came into its eyes. Then she turned away from it shut the door and methodically started folding the clothes.

She worked faster soon and more confidently; an amiable able woman. And steady. Lady Fletcher, a woman of title, —wife of the judge.

5   *The Weeping Child*

'Well, I have seen a ghost,' said Mrs Ingham, 'and it was the ghost of someone who is still alive.'

Then she got up and left them, putting down her knitting on a cane chair and walking off rather bent forward and clenching her rheumaticky hands. She was a big old woman with a large jaw and determined mouth, white hair screwed back anyhow, but eyes quite gentle. She visited her daughter in Jamaica—a lawyer's wife—in their beautiful great house in the mountains above Kingston harbour every other year at the end of January after the marmalade. The late spring was impossible because of the spring-cleaning and seeds, the summer because of the watering and the autumn because of the fruit. She lived in Surrey, England, in a sensible modern house the far side of Guildford near the arboretum and had two acres of garden. She was a J.P., a speaker for the W.I. and had been a keen Girl Guide until nearly sixty. Her long and expensive bi-annual flight above the Atlantic Ocean, moving her ten miles further from Surrey every minute, yet one hour back in time every thousand miles, she passed very steadily. Pipes had been lagged, stop-cocks manipulated, Christmas thank-you letters all disposed of, the tree tidily burned in the bonfire place. Keys had been hung labelled at strategic points and her will left conspicuous in case of hi-jack or engine trouble. The dahlias were safe under straw and excellent arrangements had been made for the cat. On the aeroplane she spoke to no one, some-times looked out of the window and often at her watch, and dropping down and down at last through the bright air to the coconuts and coral and the wonders of her daughter's house which stood in a spice plantation and smelled night and day of incense, she lost no time in measuring her grandchildren for knitted cotton vests which they never dreamed of wearing.

But, 'Yes, I have seen a ghost,' she said.

'Where's she gone?' asked her daughter's husband, turn-ing round with the decanter.

Her daughter blinked. It was late in the evening. She was great with a fifth child. It was astonishingly hot for the time of the year and their dinner guests wouldn't go.

Also her mother tired her. Not physically. Mrs Ingham had never had any wish to be taken about or entertained or shown the tourist attractions. Most days they just sat on the verandah together, with the smaller children flop-ping around them, the newest baby under its net wailing now and then until a servant came silently up with its bottle. Mrs Ingham required less physical effort than most visitors.

It was her simple presence that was tiring—her endless, sensible, practical conversation—committee meetings, local elections, deep-freezes, the failure of cabbages, the success of jam, the looking at the watch and saying, 'Isn't it time we started on the school-run now, dear?' or, 'If dinner's at nine, you'll want them to have the lamb in the oven by eight. I will see to the mint sauce.'

When guests arrived Mrs Ingham sat back, never trying to hold the floor, never conspicuous. Sensibly she had taken great trouble from her first visit to find out about clothes. 'Never sleeveless!' the dressmaker in Guildford had said, looking at Mrs Ingham's sinewy arms. 'Oh yes—everyone,'

Mrs Ingham had said, 'tailored and pure cotton and quite short. And always sleeveless.'

'But just imagine! In January!'

Mrs Ingham hadn't been able to imagine it either. Imagining was her rarest occupation. But as Miranda had said before her first visit that it would be hot, she had taken care to find out how hot, to look at books and brochures and magazines and Philips' Modern Atlas. She had a reverence for properly checked facts and had been for many years an examiner of Queen's Guides. Thus at her daughter's dreamy and romantic dinner parties she sat unselfconscious and correct.

Miranda said to her husband sometimes as they lay in their four-poster bed and listened to the tree-frogs in the night, 'I wish she'd go.'

'Why?' he said, 'I like your mother.'

'She wears me out.'

'Wears you out! She just sits on the verandah.'

'She wears me out with guilt. She makes me feel fifteen again—not helping with the weeding.'

'But there isn't any weeding.'

'She's so rational and busy.'

'Well you don't have to be rational and busy.'

'She makes me feel bored all over again.'

'Come on,' he said, dropping an arm over her, 'you've left home now.'

'One doesn't,' she said, 'ever. And anyway she bores other people.'

'Don't be horrible,' he said, 'you miss her like hell always, after she's gone.'

Miranda was right in one thing, though, for Mrs Ingham did bore people sometimes, especially when Miranda herself was self-conscious about her mother's ordinariness and fell silent too. 'I am weighted down,' she thought tonight. She ran her hand over the new baby beneath her long dress and sighed. They were all sitting after dinner on the lovely pale verandah with the long eighteenth-century drawing-room stretching behind it and the shadows of the servants here and there in the windows or on the lawns in the hot night under the stars. The guests were a heavy lot. The dinner hadn't been the best she'd ever offered. The lamb, having been put in at eight, had been over-cooked when they sat down at ten which was of course what nine meant in Jamaican. Stephen had asked some Fillings of extraordinary deadliness—friends of friends of friends in London and a handsome but silent barrister. And there was an English judge's wife, quite a nice looking woman but with little to say. The other couple— two of their Jamaican friends—were beautiful and fashion-able and cheerful, usually very cheerful. Great drinkers and laughers when the four of them were together. Witty. Hilarious. Not tonight.

The conversation had reached the stage when people were saying that coffee smells better than it tastes and Miranda shut her eyes.

'Wasn't this a coffee plantation once?' asked Mrs Filling.

'Coffee and spices,' said Stephen. 'The coffee beans were spread out upon the square—the place that looks like a school yard over in front of the guest house.'

'Was the guest house . . .?'

'Yes—slave quarters. They kept fifty slaves here once.'

'What, here? Just here?'

'That's it,' said Stephen. 'We keep the chains under the beds.'

'*Do* you?' gasped Mrs Filling.

'Is it haunted?' asked the judge's wife.

B*

'Sure,' said Stephen. 'You hear the groans and screams all night. Lashings and floggings. It's good for getting rid of guests. Nobody stops long.'

'I'm sure *I've* never heard anything,' said Mrs Ingham, knitting away, and with a sinking heart Miranda heard the conversation turn to ghosts. 'In a minute,' she thought, 'someone will say, "Isn't it funny—you never meet anyone who's actually seen a ghost—always it's a friend."' 'When they say that,' she thought, easing her heavy self about in the chair, 'I shall scream and scream and run round the house and take a machete out of a woodshed and come back and chop everybody's head off.'

'Isn't it odd,' said the judge's wife, 'you never meet anyone who's in fact seen a ghost. Always . . .'

'But everyone believes in them, you know. We all believe in them,' said someone—the barrister, Robert Shaw.

'I don't see why we shouldn't believe in them,' said the Jamaican lawyer. 'I just don't see why we're supposed to find them interesting.' Miranda smiled at him.

'Oh, I think they are. I think they are,' said Mrs Filling and then sank back in her chair and said no more for the rest of the evening. Mr Filling cleared his throat. Miranda thought, my God, a ghost story.

'The trouble with ghost stories,' she said, 'is they're so long. Who'd like more coffee?'

'And Lady Fletcher's right,' said Stephen, 'no one has ever seen a ghost himself. It's always the other feller's, too much of it and the mixture as before.'

It was then that Mrs Ingham said, 'I have seen a ghost,' and getting up to leave them said, 'it was the ghost of someone who is still alive.'

'I thought I heard the children,' she said coming back.

She picked up her knitting and sat back in her chair. 'I was wrong. No. Now. It is a very short story and not I think usual. I saw the ghost of a weeping child. It was standing in the corner of a greenhouse in an old kitchen garden. It was a boy. Eight years old.'

'Oh, I'm sure this country is full of ghosts,' said the judge's wife comfortably.

'This was not Jamaica,' said Mrs Ingham, 'it was at home in Surrey. It was just outside Reigate. Last summer.'

'Ma,' said Miranda, 'are you all right?'

'It was on August the twentieth—a Wednesday—at three o'clock in the afternoon. It was the house of people I don't know. I had been told that the woman might lend the house for a Red Cross function and I had gone over to see if it would be suitable. When I got there I was given a cup of tea and was shown round and saw at once that the place would be most *unsuitable*. There were imitation daffodils in a Ming vase and an indoor swimming pool. Very vulgar. No windows open and a fur sofa! I saw only the housekeeper who was a slut and kept a television set going—with the sound turned down—the whole time I was with her. All the time I talked she looked at it. She could hardly find her mouth with her cigarette.

'When I got up to go she said, "They said you'd want to see the gardens."

' "No thank you," I said.

'Then, when I got into the drive again I saw that the gardens were very much the best things there, and round the corner of a rose garden—beautifully kept—I thought I saw a kitchen garden wall. Now I am very fond of kitchen gardens and I said that I thought I would change my mind. "I will have a quick look about," I said and there was no need for her to accompany me.

'Well, round the end of the rose garden things were not

so promising. There was a stable block, very broken down. Empty loose boxes put to no use. But I walked on a little and found a gate in a red wall and through it a really excellent kitchen garden. An *excellent* place. Beautifully kept. Huge. I could see the gardener bending over some beans at the far end and the wall beyond him was covered in the most splendid peaches and the wall at right angles to it—to the peach wall—had one of the longest conservatories I have ever seen running along it, in a private house. Long enough for—two or three hundred tomato plants, I dare say. But oh, very battered and un-painted, very broken. Inside there was an old stone path stretching away down it with moss in the cracks and a huge vine with a bulging trunk, running everywhere. Miles and miles of it. In all directions. Beautifully cared for. The numbers on the bunches had been pruned out marvel-lously. I walked the whole length of the greenhouse, look-ing up into the branches and the dozens and dozens of bunches—it was a little white grape—like so many lan-terns. Glorious. It was hot and steamy and good manure on all the roots, and the smell of greenhouse—delicious—very strong.

'And so quiet. I was admiring the vine so much and it was so quiet and the air so heavy and still that I felt, well really quite reverent. Like in a church. I walked all the way down the greenhouse and all the way back gazing up above my head.

'And then, when I was nearly back to the door again I heard a child crying and saw that there was a little boy standing near the tap in the corner. He was sobbing and weeping dreadfully. As if his heart was quite broken. I went up to him and talked to him and tried to stop and comfort him but he paid no attention. He was in leggings and a shirt and he had red hair. He had his fists in his eyes and just stood there beside the bright brass tap and the more I spoke to him the more he wept and turned away from me.

'So I went out and said to the gardener who was still down at the end of the gardens with the beans that there was a boy crying in the greenhouse and he said, "Oh aye. It's me."

'I begged his pardon.

'He said, "It's me, ma'am. I'm often there. People are often seeing me."

'But I said, this was a child. Not more than nine.

'He said, "Eight, ma'am. I was eight," and he got up off his haunches and eased his back and looked at me with that look Scotsmen have. A sandy, grizzly-haired man. Tall. Abrupt. He was about seventy years old. A straight sort of a man. And a bit of an old stick, I should say. He didn't mind whether I believed him or not.

' "I was wrongfully accused," he said, "for something I never did. I'm very often there." Then he got down on his haunches again and went on picking beans and flinging them in handfuls into a chip basket.

'I went off back to the greenhouse but the child was not there any more. The tap was there, perhaps not so bright —and the vine was just the same—the rough, pale, splintery trunk, the dark leaves above. The light seemed different, though, and it was not so quiet.'

'Go on,' said Stephen. 'Ma—do go on.'

'That is all,' said Mrs Ingham. 'That is the story.'

'But didn't you go back?' said Miranda. 'Go back and ask him more?'

'What more?'

'Well—what it was he'd done? Whether he'd done it?'

'Oh, he hadn't done it. I rather think he'd forgotten what it was all about. I had that feeling. He certainly hadn't done anything wrong.'

'How could you be sure?' asked Robert Shaw.

'Oh, the weeping,' she said, 'it was the weeping. It was not remorse or anger the weeping. It was—well, tremendous disappointment and bitterness and sorrow. A sort of'—she wrinkled her sensible forehead—'it was a sort of essence of sorrow. Like a scent. A smell. Something very heavy and thick in the air.'

In the silence that followed she said, nodding round brightly, 'We ought to be so *careful* when we advise children. It's quite frightening what we do.'

'You never told me,' said her daughter, 'why ever didn't you tell me about it?' and she felt the usual dismal guilt confronting her mother's open face and with it an unusual violence and resentment. Ridiculously—her Jamaican friends looked at her in surprise—she thumped the chair arms. 'You might have *told* me that story. I should have been *told*. Why didn't you *write it* to me?'

'D'you know, I just can't say.' Her mother wound up her knitting and stuck the needles through the ball of wool. 'In a way I just seem to have remembered it.' Her voice, cool and self-reliant and thoughtful, left Miranda excluded.

'You might have *told* me.'

'But, dear, it seemed so—well, so ordinary at the time. Whatever time, of course—' and she gave her most sensible Queen's Guide smile, 'whatever time of course it was.'

The House Above Newcastle

Oh she was a pretty girl, Catriona (that's Pussy) Fox-Coutts. That's to say, Fielding now. Pussy Fielding. Pussy Fielding nearly a week. Boofie was always rather an eye-catcher, too—Boofie Fielding, Henry and Adelaide's boy. The Guards. Oh, they made a good-looking pair!

'Hey hey hey HEY,' said the little old man on the steps of the Pineapple Bay Hotel—five star and then some, 'here she com'. Here she com', *here* she com', here she com' NOW!' The manager, sleek as an eel—Chinese and conceited with it—knocked him round the corner. He was the old man who raked the beach and he had no business on the front steps at all in his old ship-wreck trousers and his white beard coming head-on like pins through his old blue leather face. 'Hey hey hey HEY!'

'You git. Lookin' at the girls. Git gone. Good evening, sir, good evening, ma'am. Mr and Mrs Fielding? Please sign in.'

Pussy—oh she was a pretty girl : and Pineapple Bay had seen more rich young brides than most places and richer than the English—went by him with a turned-away, sideways smile. Her new husband signed their name for the third time : Church register, Savoy (first night) and now here, Jamaica. Then he looked round and found the bell-op with his eye, nodded and went ahead of their luggage with confidence. So young! Eton and the Guards of course—but a very nice boy, Boofie Fielding. Everybody

liked him. And it had been a really good wedding—
Claridges. You can't beat Claridges—though it was a pity
it was winter. If they'd only waited until summer they
could have had it in the country. But you can't put up a
marquee in January, not in Perthshire. And marquee or
no marquee you can't expect people to come to Perthshire
in January. Not really. Not unless they're going on to
ski.

So Lady Fox-Coutts came down and stayed with her
sister-in-law in Campden Hill and they did it all from
there, and really, it *had* been a lovely wedding, especially
for the parents who had known each other for so long and
had all the same friends. They kept it almost entirely to
the army and the Fox-Couttses and Fieldings had waxed
quite noisy, greeting the procession of grand old and military faces and the bride's godfather, dear old Henry Whatsname—Argylls?—had made a touching speech about old
forgotten far-off things and battles long ago. By comparison the younger generation, what there were of them,
for it had been impossible to invite many with all the
V.I.Ps, had been on the quiet side and had left earlyish.
Just a couple of cousins had come on to the little family
dinner-party afterwards in Campden Hill where after
dinner Lady Fox-Coutts had gone out on to the covered
balcony and talked long and deliciously about Cairo and
Shepheard's to Fielding senior (Colonel) and how different
things might have been if Fox-Coutts hadn't turned up
after Tobruk.

'But it was a pity really,' she said (Pussy's mother) to
Fox-Coutts as they went to bed about two a.m., 'I'd always
planned a *summer* wedding for Puss. Why ever were they
in such a hurry? They're almost indecently young after
all.'

'Oh, and it isn't *that*, George,' she said catching her

husband's eye, the glitter above the martial nose and
bristles—rather a blood-shot glitter tonight— 'No, I'm
quite sure there's nothing like that.'

Nor was there, nor had there been, for Catriona (Pussy)
and Alexander (Boofie) Fielding had not slept together.
Meeting at a usual Kensington party stiff with gate-
crashers, bright-eyed pot-smokers in pricy rags, horse-
people and debs, semi-debs and emergent members of
Lloyds and the Inns of Court—the usual lot—they had
at once and each for the first time fallen deeply in love,
and had for nearly three months seldom been seen apart
from each other. Pussy in the last stages of Miss Catherine
Judson's Secretarial College, Collingham Road and Boofie
at Wellington Barracks had met daily—sometimes three
times daily, anywhere and everywhere and every single
evening Boofie was not on duty. Within two weeks they
had decided to marry. Within one week it had been
assumed by their friends that they must by now, of course,
be lovers. They went to some lengths in fact—though they
never discussed them with each other—to let this be
assumed and they did this not so much because to be in
love and not in bed might be considered an oddity, feeble,
a moral timidity in their particular set, but because they
wanted to keep their astonishing secret : and this was that
they were so sure of themselves that there was no particular
hurry.

Pussy considered this phenomenon often, the two and
a half months before they married, alone in bed in her
aunt's house in Campden Hill where she was living until
the secretarial course was over. It was the room she had
often had as a little girl, always known as Pussy's room
(Aunt Fox-Coutts had no children of her own) and it was
unchanged since she first knew it—the Lucy Atwells on
the walls, the Arthur Ransomes on the shelf, her old bear

on the bed. Lying on this bed, stroking the bear thought-
fully and keeping it beside her through the night, she
wondered on about whether it was odd of her to want to
wait to go to bed with Boofie.

Boofie on the other hand didn't think of it at all. He
had been to bed with several girls and had forgotten all
of them except the first who was old, and awful afterwards. Pussy Fox-Coutts had absolutely nothing to do
with all that. Discussing her with no one he simply looked
forward to her happily in every way. He had an open
though not an empty face, Boofie Fielding, and would have
been at home with subalterns a hundred years back in
some ways. If pressed it is even just possible that he would
have even said that nice girls don't do it beforehand though
of course it is different for a man. He read few novels and
was uninfluenced by the cinema. But he was more interesting than he appeared.

After Claridges the two of them had gone on to a
night-club where Pussy, in a thick, clinging raw-silk dress
and jacket from that madly expensive place in Walton
Street, had turned heads. Some escaped young from the
wedding reception had also turned up. It had grown noisy
and late. There had been a memorable bill for the champagne and Pussy and Boofie looking better and better the
more champagne they drank (they were nineteen and
twenty-one) had fallen into their bed at the Savoy and
slept at once : and the best man's—Tom Shaw's (that's
Robert Shaw's nephew—the ass that'll get the title if he
survives his Ferarri)—the best man's terribly funny joke
of ringing them at five a.m. had misfired because they
thought it was their early call for Heathrow and had leapt
out of bed at once.

Pussy said she'd stay up now because she must do something about her hair. She disappeared to the bathroom and

Alexander followed and leaned against the door and watched her lift up her thick fair hair and pin it and put a hat over it and step under the shower. When she came back he put out a hand and held on to her shoulder and she stopped unpinning her hair and looked at him.

But then it was their genuine early call, a knock at the door and breakfast. That evening they were touching the Equator at Pineapple Bay.

'That's a good-looking couple.'

Robert Shaw, lying on his chaise-longue under a striped umbrella on the beach, tapped Monique Santamarina's hand to make her look up, or rather down, for Mrs Santamarina favoured an uplifted chin nowadays. Turning vast, black glasses towards the sea she watched Pussy and Boofie splashing alongside, hand in hand, just up to their ankles and smiling around at the world. Each step made a splash of whiter-than-white foam. Pussy's bikini and Boofie's bathing trunks were as white, and her hair, swinging thick and cut expensively in a fat, thick circle shone like silver. His was dark and curly.

'They look as if they were advertising something,' said Mrs Santamarina.

'Married bliss, I'd say,' said Robert. 'It's a honeymoon advertisement. Good God, I believe it is a honeymoon advertisement! It's the great Fox-Coutts wedding. We know the aunt. Don't look at them. They're nice children and we're back in Kingston tomorrow,' and he made sure that the legal party and the Bolivians sat well apart from Pussy and Boofie at dinner, he with his back to them. This was kind but not at all necessary for Pussy and Boofie were put far off in a grotto at the honeymoon table, just under the humming-bird nectar-dip and beside the lily pool, though the waiters still couldn't take their eyes off

Pussy, and Mrs Filling, sitting rather bowed down across the table from her own munching husband, found herself unable not to peer, gazing at the distant Boofie tenderly as at filmstars of long ago. 'A honeymoon couple,' she said. Filling said, 'Honeymoon, eh?' They spooned up their mangoes, trying to like them, considering what this meant.

The waiters nearly broke in two, bowing Pussy and Boofie out, and the maid leaving their bedroom as they approached gave a fat black smile. Inside, the beds were close up together and turned down at the corners, the pillows and sheets strewn with fluffy pink cat-tails and hibiscus. There was a great vase of lilies in the room and the silent air-conditioning made it cool. Moonlight through the shutters made the shadows portentous and dark.

'Good Lord,' said Boofie, 'it's like a church.'

'Boofie,' Pussy went out on to the balcony, letting in the hot night. She looked at the black scissor curves of the palms. The sea behind them and a little below could be heard softly, and periodically flashing a slow white wave. 'Boofie, I'm terribly sorry. I'm most awfully tired.'

'Poor Pussy.' He walked over and put his arm round her but she walked back into the room, wriggled and stepped out of her long cotton dress and lay down flat on her face on the bed. 'I'm just so *tired*.'

'It's all right,' he said, 'don't worry.'

She sat up, wriggled out of the rest of her clothes, wriggled into her nightie that was laid out for her, folded up the clothes neatly and put them in a scant, tidy pile on the bedside table. Then she flopped down again and closed her eyes. 'It's all right,' he said again, coming over to her. He touched her neck with a finger but she flung away.

'It's six hours later than it is,' he said, 'for us you know. We've missed a night somewhere. The night-club was a crazy idea. You must be dead.'

Her eyes closed. He walked round the beds and got into his own. After a little while when he seemed sound asleep Pussy carefully sat up, stretched out to the bedside drawer for cold cream and carefully began to deal with her face. Then she crept to the bathroom where she removed her nail varnish, did her teeth quietly, combed rather than brushed her hair and washed as much of herself as she could with a flannel. She tidied the bathroom. Creeping back to the bedroom she collected her bear from its lopsided examination of the basket chair and wrapping it in her arms was asleep till breakfast time.

Two days later, three days later, four days later—Pussy and Boofie were down on the sleek white beach before breakfast. Then breakfast on the balcony, sugar-pink cloth, sugar-pink pointed napkins, mountainous, cornucopious basket of fruits, coffee, scrambled eggs and the table scattered with flowers. In her long, yellow beach dress Pussy sucked oranges, nibbled at mangoes and munched tiny bites of little sweet cakes. Boofie drank black coffee and messed about with the eggs.

The third day he ordered newspapers. He was not a tall young man, rather small really, and at breakfast in his bathing trunks he looked touchingly young and hairless— even younger somehow leaning back and clearing his throat and shaking out last week's *Times*. The waiters still beamed and smiled at them all the time with wide, knowing gleams. 'Now good morning, sah, good morning, ma'am. And how are you today?'

After breakfast Boofie went back to the beach while Pussy tidied everything and did her nails and her face against sunburn, or had her hair done in the hotel salon. Then a short swim—their hand-in-hand walk in the shallows had almost become a performance—and the heads of the other guests turned to them. They were rather old, American heads mostly, except for one child who was not altogether welcome on the beach because he would dig holes in it. Again and again he was having to be told to stop by the old beach-raker. 'Now you just don't go digging on this beach, boy. There'll be people coming breaking their legs.'

'Poor boy,' said Pussy, 'fancy a beach like this and not being allowed to dig in it,' and she left Boofie to swim out to the coral reef and helped Ned build a great Norman castle with a huge deep moat. The beach-raker hung about muttering to himself, only quieted by the occasional smiles Pussy threw like presents to the stone on which he sat apart.

They slept in the greatest heat of the day and in the afternoons bathed again; then changed for dinner, slowly, talking all the time, on her part, about the wedding—the guests, the presents, the new flat. She talked and talked of the flat—it was almost a house really, a mews house near Stanhope Gate. Most *super* luck and a marvellous investment. 'Your father's an absolute honey,' she kept saying. 'Oh, I do hope they have the sense to do the floor properly in the sitting-room. I suppose Mummy'll have the sense—'

'She'll be there,' said Boofie. ' Don't worry.'

'I'd like to have seen to getting the kitchen finished. I'm not sure if they understand about the cooker.' (She had done the three month Cordon Bleu between school and Miss Judson's and was serious about technicalities.)

'We've all our lives,' he said coming up behind her at the dressing table, 'for choosing cooking stoves.'

'But it's important. It's important. I mean, now you've left the army—now you're working' (he'd joined Courtauld's) 'you'll be home each evening. It's got to be *right*. We'll be having a lot of people.'

He put both hands on her shoulders and put his face against the warm top of her head.

She said suddenly, 'Boofie—I don't think I'm going to be able to manage.'

'You fool,' he said, turning her round, making her stand up, holding her tight. But there was a knock on the door and it was some painted Americans all dressed in whites from tennis, she with a little red bow in her white hair and little red bows in her tennis shoes to match—some Americans to ask them to do them the honour of coming out to dinner with them in Montego Bay.

That night—the fifth night—it was three a.m. Pussy took up the bear almost in a daze, a trance, as she fell on the bed. 'I'm terribly sorry, darling. I'm dying. I'm dead. I'm asleep.'

But she got up again this time while he was still awake to put things to rights. She even had a shower and used the noisy hair brush. She washed her underclothes and creamed her face in the bathroom, calling through, 'This cream's made out of avocado pears.' Folding and tidying the thick pink towels she said, 'D'you know, I think I'll go mad if they've not done the parquet when we get back.'

But taking up the bear again, again she fell on the bed on her face. 'Oh, I'm so terribly sorry, darling. I'm so tired.'

He said nothing now. He was awake and lying on his back with his arms behind his head. It was rather a small head with a stern look of propriety and duty about the nose. If he hadn't been beautiful he might have been dapper. But no—even had he not been beautiful he would have been better than dapper. He had ease about him, like an animal. But an interesting animal. His black hair curled faun-like and thick. It was right that he had left the army.

'All right,' he said. He lay still for a long time after she slept looking at the ceiling, watching the silent whirling electric fans, listening to the shrieks and love songs of the tree frogs in the ornamental bushes tastefully planted in a measured semi-circle around the grassy sweeps and artificial crescents of the hotel forecourt.

They woke to rain—warm splashes of rain that increased to torrents, swept onto the balcony, soaking the pink cloth, the plastic chaises-longues. Waiters carried everything into the room and they ate damp bread and wet fruit and watched lightning and purple rolls of cloud like smoke come down and blot out the sea. 'It's never for long,' said Boofie, 'get ready and we'll go somewhere.'

'Oh yes. All right.'

'We'll go off in the car somewhere. Doesn't matter where. Inland. Not Montego Bay. The rain'll stop soon. We'll get up into the mountains.'

'It'll stop soon,' he announced to the Chinese eel on the hotel steps, waiting for a man to bring round their hired car. 'Oh yes,' said the eel, 'it's never long.'

'Any point waiting for it to ease off? It certainly is pretty heavy.'

It was. Neither Boofie nor Pussy had seen anything like it before in their lives. In minutes, as they watched, from seeming impossible to increase, it had doubled in force, turned from a storm to a deluge, from a deluge to a massive waterfall, a turbulent lake in the air, deafening, ferocious. The hotel stood within minutes at the meeting of waters, swirling, lapping at the steps, covering the steps, slopping in trickles, in pools, in floods over the marbled indoor terraces.

'We'll wait,' said Boofie.

But then it eased. Eased and stopped.

'There'll soon be the sun,' said the old beach-raker, 'the sun'll be soon out. Here she com'.'

'Git gone,' said eel, knocking him out of sight.

They got to their car which very surprisingly started, and turned it and set off in clouds of steam. The road about them steamed, the trees, the little straw huts selling beads and baskets and expensive American clothes and jewellery. Inland, up a hill that still foamed and ran like a river, the tunnel beneath its trees still steamed. Out into sudden flashing light at the end of it, fields, woods, flowers and people steamed. Pineapples on wayside stalls blazed and steamed. Women coming wet out of the forest with babies on their hips laughed and steamed and called. A great landscape appeared, miles of dark and black-green forest, then sweeps and tilts of grass, like downs, then a sudden clutch of banana trees with shiny stems of green paper and wet green plate-like leaves of cheese plants unfurling almost as you passed, a dazzle of a white wood fence already showing sprouts of green. Burning sun. Wet grasses. Now a gliding group of coconut palms, spaced out, leaning all the same way like dancers, almost moving along in the soft rich earth. 'The trees are like—animals,' said Pussy. Boofie took a hand off the wheel to hold one of hers and she did not take it away.

But higher up in the mountains the rain began again. It announced itself first by some slaps and rattles rather like far-off guns, like firing practice, then unmistakably like thunder. Then like tremendous thunder. Lightning flickered and struck in the trees—fir trees now for they had climbed high. Lightning struck the road just to one side of them. The road was narrow and stony and very slippery. With some relief they swung into a sudden surprising town with a great piazza and a huge unlikely cliff-wall above it. 'It's Newcastle,' said Boofie. 'I wanted to see Newcastle. It's a great army place. I'd like to write something about Newcastle.'

'*Write* something?' said Pussy. She was nonplussed. 'Do you write things? I didn't know.'

'There's a lot I'd like to write about the army,' he said, 'specially now I'm out of it.'

She was looking at him. He stopped the car in the middle of the deserted piazza and looked up at the great memorial tablets fastened to the cliff above it and saw his own regimental plaque. He said, 'Look, Puss.' There was a loving, tolerant, amused look on his face. Pussy sat blank-faced and at sea, out of her depth at sea. 'I don't know him at all,' she thought, 'I just don't know what to say.'

Boofie looked down at her—or rather across because as I say he was a short man—short, though very nice-looking of course like Pussy who was a very pretty girl, even now, while trying not to cry and with rain coming in through cracks in the roof of the hired car and messing her hair and wetting her dress and thinking, 'I don't know him at all. He's too clever.' She held the bear on her knees as the rain trickled down and made a puddle in her lap. Unnerved by Boofie's unfamiliar face she suddenly wailed, 'My bear's getting wet,' in a high and petulant, nursery voice. And with sudden cold horror she saw her husband think. 'My God—she's silly.'

'We'll go on,' he said.

'Go on—but the storm's just *starting* again.'

'We'll go on.'

He re-started the car and went tearing out of the barrack square. A rending, booming crack and almost simultaneous flash of light seemed to occur about five feet in front of them on the now even steeper mountain road. The deluge blotted out the windscreen, the wipers stopped, a river rushed around the wheels.

'Booffeeeeeee!'

She heard the feeble silliness of the cry, saw Boofie's foot go harder down on the accelerator. The car swung, righted itself, swung, shuddered, righted itself, then uncannily went on up the hill through the rushing water. There was another flash of lightning, a shout of thunder, the sound of something falling in the forest.

'You'll kill us.' Pussy's voice wavered pitifully into a scream which Boofie hardly seemed to hear.

'We'll see,' he snapped and took the car round the sharpest bend yet. It was a bend that narrowed, tilted upwards turned into a dirt track and presented itself head on to a high and beetling, earthy bank armed at intervals with protruding over-sized navy-blue lilies. At this bank the car flung itself bravely, bucked, shied, momentarily stood on its back wheels and with a dying whinny fell upon its back and lay still.

Bride and bridegroom crawled out of it, Pussy holding tight to her bear.

'Run,' cried Boofie, 'there's a house.' Not waiting for her or looking to see if she followed, he ran—there was a track like a stream to the side of the bank and the wooden roof of some sort of house could be seen above.

A most curious house—a sort of Swiss chalet standing on a little alp and despite the driving, tropical, boiling rain and the great fat flowers planted at its door it was a house suggesting sharp and cleanly things—Scandinavia or Switzerland. Even snow. There was a padlock on the door which someone had forgotten to click shut. 'Come on, you fool,' Boofie roared kicking open the door.

'Boofie!' Pussy was coming. He pulled her in behind him, grabbed the bear and flung it out (it landed on a seat on the terrace) and slammed the door on it. 'And stop calling me Boofie.'

'What!'

'Stop calling me Boofie.'

'But I've always called you Boofie.'

'Always is over. Call me Alexander. And get some food.'

'Get some *food*!'

'Yes, and a dry towel!'

'A dry towel!'

'Yes. There should be a towel. It's a holiday house. Break something open. Oh hell—I'll break something open. You get some food.'

'Boofie!'

'Shut up.'

'Alexander.'

'Look—there's the kitchen. Look for some food. It's long after lunchtime. It's nearly evening. We need some food. we're wet and we're cold and we're miserable.'

'Miserable?' sobbed Pussy.

'Miserable,' said Alexander and kicked and pushed a door into the nether regions. He came back with a rough brown towel and began to dry his face and hair. When the wet had been transferred to the towel he flung it across to her.

She flung it back at him without a word and went into the kitchen and shut the door. Shortly, there was a scream followed by a crash and sounds of things breaking and she appeared at the door again holding a primus type of cooking stove with foot-high flames emerging from it.

'Fool!' bellowed Alexander again and, seizing it, slung it out of the front door where it sizzled and died among the lilies.

'I've never used one,' she wept. He looked masterfully around the kitchen. 'There's a cooker, you idiotic woman, and a calor gas cylinder if you use your eyes.' He turned a knob. 'With gas in it. I thought you were a Cordon-Bleu.'

'But there's nothing to cook!'

'There's tins. Look.'

'They're—they're baked beans!'

'Well?'

'We can't eat baked *beans*.'

'There's some pilchard things.'

'I WON'T eat pilchard things.' She was crying quite hard now and shouting in a lower and more masterful key than in the car.

But, 'You WILL eat pilchard things,' roared Alexander, '*and* baked beans. Together. On plates. There's a tin opener.' He flung out.

Later she appeared with two tin plates with food on them. They sat on the floor propped up against a vast double bed which Alexander had manufactured by heaving at the seat of what had at first appeared to be a large sofa. He had spread it with two army-type blankets he'd found, for it was still cold. And the rain still roared and splashed and swirled about the hut and lightning still lit the mountain slopes of black pines through the darkening window. The beans and fish were rather good.

She said after a while, 'Oh, Alexander.'

'Pussy,' he said, stretching out his hand.

Then, 'No, Puss leave the plates on the floor.'

'I've got my foot in one of them,' she said after a time. 'It's all bean juice.'

'I love you,' said Alexander, 'forget your feet.'

As it grew dawn she woke alone on the nobbly, rather mouldy-smelling great bed and pulling one of the hard blankets round her—from far away on the floor—walked out of the little house on to the terrace. Alexander was there. The rain had stopped and it was a clear morning— cloudless, with paling stars and already quite warm. She walked over to him and leaned herself against him and they stood together close in the blankets by the rough parapet. In the creeper that grew along it there was the little light of a firefly and with precision and tenderness he caught it and handed it to her in the darkness of his two cupped palms.

'I can't keep it,' she said, and after a minute let it go, leaning herself on him again. 'Oh I do *love* you so.'

'Come back,' he said and they went back into the house. 'No, leave open the door,' he said, 'let the light in. It's going to be a lovely day.'

It was past afternoon when they were going back, down towards the plain again. He had righted the car and made it start and she had sat and watched with adoring admiration. 'And get in,' he had said, 'stay here and get in. I'll go back and lock up, not you.'

'Did you tidy it all up?' she asked, almost asleep, heavy on his shoulder as he drove fast down through Newcastle down to the pineapples and palm trees.

'Nope,' he said, 'I just clicked the padlock.'

'But the blankets?' she said, 'and the bean plates? Did you switch off the calor—?'

'Shut up,' he said kindly, 'it had to be left like that.'

'And I left my bear,' she said sleepily, moving out of the car into the beating heat of afternoon—the glossy Americans sprang about the tennis court, a waiter in a

pink coat and with an impeccable tray of planters'
punches, balanced high, crossed the terrace.

'We wouldn't want this for long, would we?' Alexander
said, looking around at it all, and she said thankfully, 'Oh
darling, of *course* not,' as though they had known each
other for ever.

Looking at him she felt faint suddenly with love, knowing all at once what love was.

'You must have thought me such a *fool*,' she said,
stretching out her hand, as they still stood beside the
car.

He looked down uneasily a moment and said seriously,
'Look, love, I'm sorry about the bear.'

'Oh shut up,' she said, 'shut up. Oh we are so *lucky*!'
They walked solemnly and rather apart back into the
hotel.

'Hey, hey, hey, HEY,' sang the beach-raker, 'there she
go, there she go, there she GO! An' the honeymoon is
over.'

'You git,' said the eel pushing him out of sight. 'You
keep you distance. You stop you filthy talk. Always
lookin' at the girls.'

7 *Saul Alone*

Well I guess my mouth is hung open. You stop thinking of spittle. You can forget a lot in here. Thank God my eyes are right.

So we're arriving here again on the beach. Not that we'd be likely going any other place. Ruthie's ahead in her long blue robe. She's chosen the table, directing the boys. They shake out the long chairs—how bright their waiters' jackets —arrange her books, belongings, the sun-tan oil. How beautiful she is, every wave of her hair in place, silver and blue like her eye-lids. She points here and there with her painted fingers. She's just had them painted at the hotel shop. When she had her hair done. Her toe nails, too. Perfect work. Like the paint on her face. She has a steady hand there still, and nearly eighty. She's a perfect piece of art is Ruthie. Well, thank God I got eyes.

So I'm down. Out of the wheeler. They've helped me down on to the long chair. She's dabbed my mouth, quick, with a handkerchief. So I *was* dribbling. From the left side of the mouth that I don't feel. The left side. The lost side. Look at the left hand, wizened up, a claw, bruised over with marks. Photographs of father. Sepia ink.

How she goes on, Ruthie. How she holds forth. I always loved hearing her talk. I switch off now when I feel like it. Well, I guess I always did. There's a lot I never told Ruthie being a silent man by nature an' liking better anyway to listen to her voice.

But the way she goes on.

For over fifty years. How many months and minutes and hours and years of fifty years has her voice gone clacketing on? From before she opens her eyes in the morning till she stretches to put out the light. 'Now then, *Saul*,' 'See here, *Saul*,' 'I've figured there's only one way, Saul.' 'Well I make my face my fortune, Saul. It's as good a way to pass the time as any.' 'I gotta make my social life my business, Saul.' On, on, on, on, on, on, on, on, on, on, on, on, on, on. 'That's the secret of happiness now we're retired, Saul. That's what it's all about.'

Why didn't she get the stroke?

I was the calm one. I always kept quiet. I never reckoned on what was right to say, so I just kept quiet and watched the figures. And joined the right clubs—golf, sailing. Bought up the right places, the right real estate, the real right estate, the right royal estate, the hotel suites and the diamonds.

Why she wear diamonds on the beach? Like a bloody Bolivian. Why I never put her straight on diamonds on the beach? Too late now.

Let me watch myself as I put out my right hand to cover her hand as she talks and talks. 'Drinks at eleven, lunch—club sandwiches—at twelve. Yes, dear, what is it? Oh look at him now, Robinson. He's holding my hand. Well, what do you know! Isn't he the old beau then? And back up to the room at twelve-thirty. Now you better not be late, see?'

Dollars from white hand into black hand. No, from pink-brown hand into fawn hand. Behind the beach-waiter stands the beach-raker. He has blue hands—and blue old chin with silver bristles coming out. He has silver shredded trousers and silver shredded toes. Not painted silver like Ruthie's but silver like fish scales, ridged and

C

horny fish scales and sand in grains along the nails' three skinward sides.

If my eyes magnified, the grains would be globes, ranged along the ridges of the great toe, each grain a silver world. To a fly— A fly's great blackberry eye regards overlapping worlds, confuses him, excites him. What does a fly see? Thank God I see. God, take not the sight of thy servant Saul, let not, as for Thy prophet Isaiah, the house be filled with smoke.

'Isn't he wonderful?'

She's asking people. It strengthens her to hear them agree with her. Some people have come up. They are very young. They have young legs. Lying so low down here it is easiest to look at their legs. No hardship neither. The girl's legs are long and bare and thin and gold and silken-looking with the coloured sea behind them. Her toe nails are painted, too, but not like Ruthie's. They are pale and gentle-coloured, hardly coloured at all, and there are silver globes of sand in them, too, and galaxies in the hollow bases between the toes, and milky ways in slanting dry patches down the legs.

Behind her lovely legs I see a castle growing with a boy and a bucket. The boy is about seven. That's David's age. The head like David's head. Like David's head was. David must be all of fifty now. The back of David's head now has a curved, broad sausage of flesh between the neck and the crown. This minute he's sweating the New York April through at the desk that's mine. Where the lightning struck.

'Look, he's trying to speak. What is it, Saul, now? He's eighty, you know. Oh yes, sir. He's been a wonderful man.' (Seems I'm dead.) 'One thing I knew at the start : he was a wonderful man.' (Oh, Ruthie, Ruthie, lay a wreath on me.)

The legs of the two young shift and they convey little sideways heaps of sand into mountain ranges with their silvery feet. Dead embarrassed.

'Did you ever see such eyes?' Ruthie holds her two hands round my live hand. 'Aren't they blue? They're blue as the day I married him—'

Shortly these kids going to be sick.

'—and I'd swear he sees as clear yet. You can see these two wonderful young people can't you, Saul? Aren't they lovely young people? They're on their honeymoon you know. HONEYMOON, hon. Yes.

'You know his eyes were always terrible important to him. Long before this happened. All his life it was eyes, eyes. You'll have heard of the pictures? That's right. Yes he did. He founded the whole collection. Yes and he chose the most of them—of the early ones. And whatever he chose—what*ever* he chose—I just always agreed with him. Not that I was ever exactly over-powered by any of them much, but I always made a big point of *saying* I liked them.'

(Seems I'm deaf.)

'That was the secret of our whole marriage. Now let me give you two lovely young people a word of advice if you want a marriage to go on like ours—it's fifty-six years —just *enthuse. En*thuse. About each other's *en*thusiasms, see? Tell you the truth, half the pictures meant as much to me one way up as the other but I always *en*thused. Well, I just used to go mad about them.'

(As a post.)

'The Gauguin—oh, sure, we still got one Gauguin—I don't know what I thought about it. But I just went wild when he said he'd got it. Tell you what, when I saw his face all lit up when he came in that night, and him standing there in the hall smilin' away and runnin' a finger over something or another on the hall table—little bit of stone, it'd be, or jade or something for holding down letters, when I saw his smilin' face, Ruthie, says I, whatever it is, *enthuse*.

'Mind, I think he still sees now. Oh I do. I think he sees all right. The eyes haven't changed. They seem to think the hearing's gone, just about. He doesn't often seem to be listening now. And of course the speech is gone. But he knows I'm here of course.'

What in hell's the beach-raker saying to that boy? Look at him straddled there, finger wagging at the kid. That's it. He don't want him digging on his new-raked beach. Holy Mike, he's saying he'll cause accidents, he'll make the old gentleman fall in the hole when he comes down for his swim. They're out of their minds. I'm not going for any swim. Kid's lower lip comes forward. Pulls his arm back to get hold of bucket. Bucket full of water for the moat. Kid not budging. That's it, David boy, go for him, water him. You stick to your position. Look at that scruff beach-raker rollin' like a bull. 'You don't go spoilin' my beach now, boy,' and pointing at me. 'Don't you go putting about the poor old gentleman.' Kid's face dead face stony face. Fingers tighten on bucket as bride's brown legs run quick and light over the beach. Clean soles of bride's feet, pale, smooth, no line on them. Left, right, little narrow feet, triangular neat heels like a baby's. Jule's feet. Jule's feet forty years old now. Once I held both Jule's baby feet in one hand. Poor Jule with her black moustache. Nearly kills her mother the black moustache.

The bride's got down by the boy now and under the very flames of the beach-raker's breath she's beginning to dig deep and wild into the satiny beach. 'You *have* to dig if it's a beach,' she says. Clear voice, young, high. Ruthie's voice a lower voice. Women's voices go lower in middle age, then higher, sillier when old age takes hold. Ruthie nearly eighty but not an old voice. A strident voice. It always was a strident voice—a grand voice, a strong voice, a quick-thinking New York voice. Good Ruthie, grand Ruthie. She's leaning towards me now. She'd never leave me. Drop me in clean dead chrome and glass, full of nurses. Look at the diamonds and the dark red nails, the lotioned, pampered hands still plump, softened by all the creams and bottles and the brown spots, the death spots, the churchyard spots (stop) faded out daily by that paste in the white jar. She's leaning with the god-awful hand-kerchief again.

Yes. Yes. We do still have one Gauguin. We had three once, boy. I gave one to Ruthie and she gave it to David. David put his right back in the collection. He'll sell it the minute I'm gone. Jule's still got hers. She'll not sell hers. Not unless she has to and she'll not have to while I'm alive. Except that I can't help her now. Not with money. David having power of attorney even though his mother . . . And I can use my right hand. Oh God get me out of here. Get me out. Free me and my right hand. Get me out so I can feel my left cheek and my crooked mouth and my dead side. Look, look all of you at the strength of my right hand.

God, I'm crying again. I don't want to cry.

'He's upset. No, no, it's all right. He does this. Now, don't you get upset, Saul. I'm here, Saul. Here, hold my hand. There . . . Don't get like that. We've got to get firm with you, the doctor said when you get like that. Honey . . . don't . . . Look, I guess you'd better go away, young man. Join the boy and dig the beach. I guess you remind him of . . . Good of you to come over. Kind of you to come over and talk to a couple of old fogeys. There,

Saul, there. Look, here's a drink now. Let me give you the cup. Fresh orange juice, Saul. There. Drink it down.'

How she goes on.

Drink it down. I never could stop her saying drink it down. Like diamonds on the beach. I never all these years have been altogether sure what I think of Ruthie.

You could always hear her voice. Right across the room. A strong voice, good and strong. An unconquerable voice. Nothing will ever get the better of that voice. That was the first thing I ever thought about her.

Neither sorrow nor weeping

Neither sickness nor dying

Nought shall separate us from the—

Like poor old Job. He recovered. In the depth of his age he recovered. He had seven more sons and three more daughters, a new life, more lands, more honours. And in all the land were no women found more fair than the daughters of Job.

After this lived Job an hundred and forty years.

Oh Ruthie, you do go on so. (The fear of the Lord that is wisdom)—with your beautiful painted old mouth and your immaculate little clean imitation teeth. (And to flee from evil, that is understanding.)

They are getting me up now and dropping me back in the wheeler and pushing me to the edge of the sea. The boy springs up and stands to. The bride springs up and stands to—then runs over and walks beside us and I gangle and droop at the sea. The old beach-raker's behind us watching. Is he sorry for me? Is he watching Ruthie's diamonds? Is he thinking that the orange juice I've scarcely touched could feed his whole family—the price of it—for a day? Maybe a week. What's he thinking there behind me? 'Poor old bastard. But he's had a great time. Yes sir. He's been a great feller times past. Millionaire. Million-

millionaire. But he got caught up with now, oh yes man!'
God—I wish I could get out.
We're at the sea's edge now. They want me to kick off
my slipper and dabble my foot. I'm nearly walking when
the chap holds me up—the left side. See Ruthie bobbing!
But I'll fall—the fools—if I dabble my foot.
So here I come, back over the beach you mustn't spoil,
the beach kept all smooth and useless for the likes of me.
For it's the likes of me that can pay to have illusions. The
likes of me who's kept so quiet, who's always watched
the figures, who's seen to it that he's been seen in the right
places. A heavy feller.
But thank God for eyes.
Gauguin had no illusions. Gauguin's beaches were tram-
melled and tracked with crabs, trenched by boats, fisher-
men and girls ran and sat heavy and still on them or
worked on them on hard orange feet. There were swirling
marks of nets, like the lashing tails of monsters, the nets
themselves spread to the sun like flowers in coloured peaks
and hollows; sand churned up now and then by the hooves
of little horses, dark horses on the pink and orange earth
down on to the luminous sand to the edge of the astounding, sounding sea.
And the horizon of the sea would be peaked and broken
like the lines of the nets. No horizon is a single line, it is
tipped and broken if you look at it closely. Triangles.
Splinters. Light. Oh, use your eyes, use your eyes, children
of God.
Yes, I do have one Gauguin, young man.
And I do still have my eyes.
But, oh God, I wish I could get out.

8 *The First Declension*

Except in colour—for it had lost a little light—Anne
Shaw's fair hair was like a girl's. It was curly and roved
about her head in pretty tendrils. It was short and she
often ran her long fingers through it as she sat eagerly
talking, for her manner was still a girl's in some ways, too,
and you could see exactly how she had been seventeen
years ago at twenty when Shaw met her—tall and slender
and rich, looking down at him from a horse near Basingstoke where they had both been invited by friends for the
week-end. She was eager and English and good.

Shaw was English and good, too, and tall and rich.
Not eager exactly. Witty and able and popular. A suitable
marriage. Really a quite remarkable marriage. A wedding
of such appropriateness that people still remembered it for
they had toasted their solidarity there, their very existence.
There had been kissing between uncongenial cousins and
the lion if it had not quite lain down with the lamb had
exchanged its address.

People particularly remembered how the bride had joy-
ously waved her arms about at everybody as Shaw had
roared them both off in an open M.G. down her father's
laurel sweep, through the stout stone gateposts to the
honeymoon (charmingly old-fashioned) in Antibes.

But Anne was no hedonist. The horse at Basingstoke had
been misleading. She was far from self-indulgent and
had had a Scotch mother and nurse and a childhood

in Edinburgh. Her father had been a lawyer. After a careful English boarding school she had gained honours in Domestic Science at Atholl Crescent. Then Basingstoke.

They lived now in London (Campden Hill) in a house as open and bright as Anne. She had it cream throughout —no William Morris or potted plants or Kensington Vic —and had imported into it a great many expensive but not showy, labour-saving machines. Its kitchen faced the street unashamed and you could see into it even late at night, blazing with fluorescent bars, because she never drew the blinds. Across the narrow, paved front garden— bulbs folded down into elastic bands the minute the flowers were done, bay trees, tubs and chains—you could view the planes of shining cupboard tops and cupboard doors and the big, Harrods, plastic-topped table, easy to clean. On one wall was an acreage of peg-board with notices pinned to it saying things like School tea-party 3.30 24th. Alison N.B. Betty fetch P. and A. Ask Polly music, B. & H. 25th. N.N.B. FOOTBALL BOOTS. Liberal Committee Meeting 7.30 28th. Do sandwiches. Behind criss-cross tapes on one bit of the board were several lots of theatre tickets—stalls—well in advance, Mrs Abbott the daily's weekly ten pound notes, an envelope for green-shield stamps, an envelope for free offers through the door and—right in the middle—three pages from exercise books each headed with a child's name and beneath each name a homework timetable. Alison's—Alison had just started at Frances Holland—showed a lot of Latin on it, and it was Latin that was the subject of discussion one December evening when Anne and Robert Shaw sat at the kitchen table for all the world to see, Anne squeezing lemons for tomorrow's dinner-party pudding.

'You mean it'd be the *Latin* that stopped you?'
c*

'Oh darling,' she said, 'it's not the Latin. It's the rest as well. I mean when it comes down to it—'

'Down?' he said.

'Well when it comes down to it who *would* do the Latin?'

'Alison would do the Latin. She'd do her own bloody Latin.'

'She can't. She loathes it. They've got a lousy mistress. I've told you. Look, Robert, if you don't get a good start in Latin you might just as well give up.'

'Perhaps *give* up.'

'Robert, look. If she doesn't get Latin she'll not get into a decent university.'

'Perhaps she doesn't want—'

They looked round because Alison had appeared to hang her schoolbag over the back of her breakfast chair, ready for morning. Buttoned neatly into her blue dressing-gown and properly slippered, she looked at them coolly. Her face was like her mother's but paler—the face of a child who drinks a good deal of milk. She might well require her university to be decent.

'Mummy says she won't come to Barbados with me,' said Robert, 'because she's got to help you with your Latin.'

'It's not the Latin,' said Anne. 'It's not only the Latin. But look. There are three of them. At school. Every day. Fetching and dropping.'

'Two,' said Robert. 'It's time Allie fetched and dropped herself. And anyhow you're on a rota. If you did extra now or when we came back someone'd do yours while we were away. Come *on*. You could come just for a couple of weeks. You needn't be there the whole two months.'

'And who would look after—'

'Anne, stop it. You could get someone. You could get your—old nurse or someone.'

'Too old.'

'And there's Ninni.'

'Ninni!'

'Or, well, someone from an agency. Or they could go to friends and we could shut the damn house up.'

'Yes and have everything pinched. I'd have to put all the silver in the bank and—'

'Well other people do.'

'Oh, it isn't worth it. Honestly, *is* it worth it?' She looked appealingly at him—she had a long and rather bending neck and it waved forward as she propped her narrow face between her hands, her hands on arms and elbows. She wriggled her shoulders about and smiled.

He said after a moment, 'Oh all right.'

'Well, is it, darling? *Is* it worth it? For a few weeks. I mean we'll be able to go away together soon. When they're a bit older (Alison, go to bed) it'll be easy. Everyone says it goes awfully fast. All of a sudden they're grown up and gone.'

'If they were at boarding school—' he said.

'I won't have them at boarding schools. I *won't* have them at boarding schools. You hated boarding schools. I hated boarding schools. We've always said.'

He got up from the table quickly and said, 'Oh well. I've got work to do.'

'What, now? It's way past nine.'

'It's got to be done.' He grinned at her from his six foot two. 'Anyway, you're still cooking.' What had been a neat, harlequin face when young—triangular with black shiny hair and rather a red mouth—had improved with age and fading corpuscles. His eyes now had the sharp and rather merry look that some lawyers' eyes get with time.

'Lawyers get sexier with age,' Anne's friend Betty Beech said one day some time later, staring into her Nescafé at Anne's kitchen table where they had been licking Liberal stickers together. 'I read it in the *Observer*.'

'I thought they were supposed to get less,' said Anne carefully.

'No. More. But they get scales on their heads.'

'Scales!'

'From wearing wigs.'

'Mine hasn't got scales. Has yours?'

'I haven't looked.'

They giggled and wriggled though it was not the sort of conversation Anne felt easy with. Harrogate and Scotland were strong and Betty was all of forty-five, her husband a top silk in Chancery.

'D'you think Lord Justice Fletcher has scales on his head?'

'D'you think he's getting sexier with age?'

'I'd have said he could hardly get less.' More laughs.

Later on though—

'He's going on this thing too, I think,' said Anne. 'This thing Robert's going to in Barbados or Jamaica or somewhere. I think Enid Fletcher's going too—I believe she's gone ahead. I really rather adore her.'

'Adore?'

'Yes. She's—oh, innocent. Quaint. Nice to be with.'

'Well, go too,' said Betty, 'you go. I'll have the children. You go, Anne. It'd do you good.'

'Oh I can't.'

'Why?'

'Oh—homework and stuff. Latin. The Fletchers have no children.'

'It's the scales on his head,' said Betty.

But she rang up that night and said again, 'You ought

to go, Anne. It's a long time to be away. For a man.'

'Oh, I know *that* will be all right,' said Anne embarrassed.

It was bad though, turning away from the barrier at Heathrow as Robert's back disappeared. His luggage had slid out of sight like a cremation. He had picked up his brief-case and then put it down again and kissed them all once more. Then he had gone. She had turned round at once, buffeting through the queue of rich Jamaicans standing like tall princes in beautiful English suits, unhurriedly looking at gold watches, brown fingers with gold rings, their women with them, tall too, but rounded, easy, fat, sweet-lipped, in plump furs. Anne grabbed a child by each hand—Andy and Polly, for Alison had started school again for the spring term—and dragged them quickly out of the first class departure lounge and over into the concrete caves of the car park. The car was on the fifth floor of it and they puffed up the stairs and stopped as Anne dropped her bag and scrabbled on the cement for the things that had rolled out. 'It's the next floor up,' said Polly. 'It's the one below,' said Andy. 'They all look the same.' In the moment of awareness that Robert had gone Andy said, 'We could be anywhere. Or nowhere. It's horrid.'

And when they found the car Anne couldn't get into it for the key kept going into the door upside down. 'Your hand's shaking,' said Polly.

'Of course it's not,' she said, and inside, fastening her safety belt, added as usual, 'see your doors are shut,' and reversed out with panache, narrowly missing a Rolls-load of Japanese who were for the moment not inscrutable.

'You're crying,' said Polly.

'Rubbish,' said Anne.

They had lunch at a Wimpy Bar for a treat, took the car home, then walked to the Science Museum and back in time to take the car for Alison.

'We could have stayed longer if it hadn't been for Alison,' said Andy, 'why can't she come home on the bus?'

'It's her first day back. If we collect her she gets home half an hour sooner.'

'Well what's so good about that?'

'She gets her homework done half an hour sooner.'

'She could do it on the bus. Anyway, why couldn't you leave us at the Science Museum? We'd be all right. Or at home with Ninni.'

'Ninni's doing the bridges of London.'

'Well, children do. Get left. You see a lot of children left in the Science Museum.'

'Well, you don't get left.'

'What's so special about us?'

'Daddy's a Q.C.,' said Anne, 'Q.C.'s children can't be too careful.'

'Why not?' said Polly. 'We're not criminals. Anyway you can't get prosecuted till you're fourteen. You just get put in care.

'And you aren't half in a jam,' she added. (They were in the impasse at the top of Sloane Street.) 'We're going to be most terribly late.'

'Then Alison will just have to wait, won't she?' said Anne, tight-lipped—and waiting Alison was, by Sloane Square tube station, their usual trysting place, with a face like thunder.

'I'd have been home by now,' she said, and uncharacteristically flung her schoolbag hard at the two young ones in the back and slammed the car door on herself. 'Why ever couldn't you have gone with Daddy?'

'Shut up,' said Andy, 'she's been crying.' He leaned

over and took his mother round the neck nearly causing a multiple incident by Chelsea Barracks. 'What nonsense,' said Anne, disengaging his arms. 'How was the Latin, Alison?'

'Fine,' said Alison, 'we've got a new woman.'

It was eight days later that Betty Beech telephoned. Anne was doing the marmalade with the au pair, Ninni.

'No—just doing the marmalade,' she said. 'Oh— January and marmalade. I suppose it'll be the same the rest of our lives. Why can't they grow marmalade twice a year? I was cutting up till midnight last night.'

'I get mine in Jermyn Street,' said Betty, ' in tins. Listen—'

'Oh you do, do you. Well you didn't do D.S. It makes you feel guilty. Though I suppose I can't grumble. I've plenty of time.'

'Yes, listen—'

'Without Robert, I mean.'

'That's what I'm trying to tell you,' said Betty, 'John's gone, too.'

'*Has* he?'

'Yes. Just as well I didn't say I'd have your children, isn't it?'

'Yes it is. I suppose you're off as well. D'you want me to have yours?'

'No thanks, I've got the girl. Anyway I've decided to go skiing.'

'Skiing! Who with?'

'Never you mind. How's Robert?'

'Oh, I haven't heard yet. I won't hear just yet. It takes ten days.'

There was a slight pause.

'Why? Don't say you've heard?'

'Oh—just the cable. And a letter he'd given someone coming back to England. To post in London. Just to say he'd arrived.'

'Pointless of course,' said Betty after another long moment. 'We'd hear soon enough if they hadn't.'

'Is John enjoying it?'

'Oh—marvellous. It sounds marvellous. Moonlight and orchids. Very hot, he says. Apparently Robert's doing some very impressive diving.'

'Oh, yes, Robert's very—'

'Snorkelling out on the reef. If I wasn't such a sucker for skiing— Well—goodbye, love.'

'Goodbye.'

'I must go for the children,' she said after a few moments to Ninni's back. Ninni had a heavy, speaking back and spent much time looking out of windows, displaying it.

After the marmalade came Andy's birthday and then Polly's birthday. January was one of Anne's big months. Robert sent greetings telegrams to each child and Anne did two enormous and faultless children's parties with lots of organised games, nothing lazy or suburban like a professional entertainer. Then there was a theatre with some friends, and dinner (people were very kind) with other friends in Hampstead. They were older friends, these, with adult children. There was even talk of grandchildren. They seemed surprised that Anne still had a child of seven and she found herself saying apologetically that she had had her children rather late, which, she thought, is really not true at all. There was only one bottle of wine too; but that was probably rather a good thing since she had to drive herself home, and it was raining. Needing petrol she found only a self-service pump in a deserted and un-

familiar part of Finchley and she draggled her long dress
running across the forecourt to pay the girl with the laconic
late-night face behind the till. If Robert had been there
the girl would have come out, she thought. She remembered the last time she'd been to dinner with the Taylors.
Robert had bought fish and chips and beer on the way
home and they had ravened at them in the car—Robert
in his new dinner jacket.

At the week-end nobody asked Anne out, or the children,
and she had planned nothing. They watched television
and went for a walk by the Round Pond on Saturday
afternoon. The trees were firewood, the wind bitter. A
black winter, not even snow. Ninni took Sunday as her
day off and spent it in bed, not even eating lunch. Anne
and the children attended the Congregational Church in
Allen Street. Afterwards the joint and Yorkshire pudding,
gravy, carrots, roast potatoes seemed rather pointless, with
excessive washing up. In the evening Anne put all the
lights on—centre light and reading lamps—in the drawing-room and sat there with Alison, but Alison was un-
communicative, lost to all human relationships in *Lord of
the Rings*.

'What about homework?'

'Done it.'

'Done the Latin?'

'Oh yes, I've done *that*.'

On Monday there was still no letter.

On Wednesday she was going to friends across the
road to dinner and was almost ready when Ninni stomped
by her in the hall, dressed to go out, too.

'But aren't you baby-sitting?'

Ninni gave her a long, Finnish look.

'Oh, Ninni! I told you I was going out.'

'It is my Class,' said Ninni.

'But you stopped your Class. You have no Class now.'

'I have it again,' said Ninni, and departed.

'Oh, no!' She flopped in a chair. Then rang the friends.

'Of course you can come,' they said. 'Alison's nearly twelve. For goodness sake! You can look in and see if they're all right after dinner if you want to. Lock them in. They're on the 'phone. The house is actually within sight—within earshot. Leave the lights on. Good gracious!'

'*Can* I go?' she asked Alison who, holding her finger in Book IV, said, 'Of course.'

She went and returning at midnight, after completely forgetting to run across and check after dinner, found everybody quite safe, Ninni returned, a hump under eiderdowns, the little ones asleep and Alison peaceful with the light on, her finger in Book VI. 'You look pretty,' she said to her mother. 'I like that silver top.'

'I like it quite,' said Anne. 'You ought to be asleep, Allie.'

'You ought to do your hair differently though.'

'Oh. And how should I do it?' She flopped down on the bed. She had had a good evening. There had been a nice man. A bit jowly but nice. He'd listened to her conversation and said things like, 'That's very true.' With a pang however she realised that he hadn't seen her across the road home. 'How should I do it?'

'Smoother,' said Alison, laying the book carefully face down before switching off the light. 'Oh, Daddy rang.'

'Daddy!'

'Yes.'

'He rang?'

'Yes.'

'But it must have cost ten pounds!'
'Twenty, I'd think. We talked for ages.'
'Allie! What did he say?'
'Oh, nothing much. I told him we were all alone. He was fed up you weren't in.'

Next morning there were two letters but over two weeks old.

Darling Anne,

We arrived at Kingston after a good flight, landing only in Bermuda to refuel. Just an hour there. We walked about the airport feeling ridiculous in jackets and ties. Most splendidly hot and a warm breeze off the sea. The sea was clear, bright green and there were feathery green trees—delicate. It was a most lovely afternoon. We took the plane on south and flew over great fields of brown stuff on the water. Like the Ancient Mariner—Wide Sargasso Sea—and at length between Cuba and Haiti, also flat and brown and dull as if nothing ever happened there! Cuba is considerably larger than I had imagined. There was a very cheerful feeling on the plane and much champagne.

Jamaica came in view with mountains and clouds and many colours. Even from a height it looks exciting and the other places nothing by comparison. We had a great reception and were installed in a fine old hotel near Kingston. It is a white, airy mansion (C18) with white balconies and big high rooms. There is a huge mango tree, tables under pale yellow umbrellas and beyond, rippling high mountains green to the very tops. I am sitting on my balcony now drinking a planter's punch and watching storms that are wandering about the mountains. You can see the lightning in the storm clouds that drift about the high valleys. But far away. There are no storms here—just hot, steady sun. We eat out of doors and very slowly and sleepily. However can anyone do any work here? The Jamaicans do—I'm sure I never could.

Below me in the lily pool I can see frogs. They have little hands and grip the sides of the pool with their fingers while getting breath to kick off again. Like people. There is a long, fat lizard on my balcony blowing his throat out at me. He is blue. His throat is green. A big black bony bird swooped down before tea and nearly got him.

Last night I couldn't sleep for the noise of the tree frogs and other amorous things in the creeper round my window.

The legal party fills nearly the whole hotel, except for some Bolivians and Brazilians and one or two business-men—faceless with faceless wives. Only the Bolivians dress for dinner. There was a woman tonight in bright pink floating silk and diamonds like a queen. We thought she must be famous—a film star—till some more came in all likewise. Well, nearly likewise. She's a bit of a particular stunner. Husbands all very short and fat and not attentive. The Bar transfixed!

With love to you all, Robert XXXX.

The second letter, a few days younger, said :

Dear Anne,

I'm sorry I haven't written again before this one. We went off on someone's yacht at the week-end and then the Conference began in earnest on Monday morning. There is a good deal of socialising—Government, Jamaican Bar, private dinner parties, etc. A lovely evening in the mountains at some ghostly old slave-house

in a spice plantation. Hostess Jamaican lawyer's wife—
English girl. Five children most of them babies. She lies
around in green pyjama things in the most beautiful
relaxed way in the world, even with six or seven to
dinner. The children run about at all hours, all in
little shifts. She has a tremendous lot of driving to do—
30 miles to school here is nothing, and back with them
all for lunch! She's having another, too, but seemed put
out by nothing, even the meat being over-cooked. The
climate I suppose. Her mother is here—told a story
about Reigate. Rather a creepy one. I must say it took a
big effort to picture up Reigate—or even England. It
feels a very long way off. Did the children get the telegrams? I love you dear. In haste R.

There is a wonderful swimming pool here. You
should see the Bolivian Queen. She 'burns on the
water'.

'Well, he did ring,' said Betty Beech. She leaned back
to get an ash-tray, then examined the two letters through
smoke, creasing her eyes. Her hair was bleached nearly
white and her face burned brown by the skiing, her eyes
very blue. She was wearing some slinky après-ski garments
though it was in fact only après-breakfast and in Paultons
Square. Anne opposite in a black macintosh looked
wrought and rather grey, perched on the edge of a chair.

'Yes, he did ring,' she said. 'Goodness knows what to say
though. I mean—after these—'

'They're not *so* bad,' said Betty doubtfully. 'Look, do
take that awful mac off. You look like a dustbin bag.
Incidentally isn't this dustbin strike thing awful? Every
street corner those awful bags. In Switzerland . . .'

'Look,' said Anne, 'look. For heaven's sake don't talk
about Switzerland. Please—you've got to tell me. Am I

right about these letters?'

'Well,' said Betty, blowing more smoke, 'they're a *little* awful.'

'They're terrible. They're terrible, Betty. They're like essays or letters we did at school on Sunday afternoons. "What I did on my Easter Holidays." Duties. And then some of the things—this Bolivian.'

'Oh, that's nothing,' said Betty, 'she's nothing. There's always one of those.'

'Or this green pyjama creature lying about in the spice plantation overcooking the meat?'

'I shouldn't worry about her either. It's not rivals. It's . . .'

'What?'

'Well,' Betty looked quickly over at her, playing for time.

'Is it the champagne that worries you?'

'No, no. Not that. That's nothing. I know Robert's not a drunk.'

'No—of course not. But,' she pointedly did not look at Anne now. For all the badinage between them they had never talked like this before and despite the après-ski and cigarette smoke Betty was not a little shaken. Anne and Robert Shaw! So open and easy and—well, sexless almost. Like brother and sister. So English. A bye-word of a rather dated happy couple. *Dear Octopus*. Anne never, never discussed Robert with anyone. Or anyone with anyone when you came to think of it. She was a sweetie, Anne; but marmalade, Latin, Harrod's socks, local politics had always seemed her boundaries.

'Perhaps her battlements?' thought Betty. She was a statement, Anne, direct and happy. She made your heart lift like a castle flying cheery flags. It was maybe all defiance.

'Have you and Robert never—? I mean, you've been married—what?—nearly twenty years. He's been away before. There must have been—?'

'Never,' said Anne. 'Never. And it's not sex that . . . I'm honestly not worried about sex. Not with Robert. It's just . . . Well it's the distance. He's at a distance.'

'He was at a distance last year in America. I know that wasn't for long . . .'

'No, no. It's the *letters*. It's the letters are at a distance. It's, oh . . .' Astoundingly she covered her face and bent her head; then sat up bravely and said, ' "Cuba was considerably larger than I had imagined." '

'Yes,' said Betty, 'yes. I see.'

'What if John wrote and told you Cuba was considerably larger than he had imagined?'

'John's never imagined Cuba at all, I don't think,' said Betty trying to lighten things. 'And he's not written to me all that much either. And he certainly hasn't rung up at twenty pounds a go.'

But Anne's eyes (good gracious) had tears in them.

'And there's something else,' she said, 'the worst thing. You've missed the worst thing.'

'What?'

' "Dear." '

'Dear?'

'Yes. "I love you, *dear*." '

'And it is sex. All right, it is sex, too,' she cried on the doorstep (Betty looked round and closed the door to the hall where her daily was washing the Spanish tiles). 'It *is* sex. I'm scared what's happening. Did John say?' she asked with a straight wide gaze, 'What did John say?'

'John said nothing at all,' said Betty, looking down. 'Except that Robert was looking much better for doing less work. The sun's doing them all good. Robert's just being his usual gorgeous self.'

'Gorgeous,' said Anne. 'Oh!'

'Stay to lunch?'

'No.' Anne was away towards the parking meter where she stood still and looked into space. Betty followed her. 'Do stay.'

'No thanks,' said Anne. 'I might be having my hair done.'

'Cut it off,' she told the hairdresser. 'Cut it as short as possible. And straighten it out and make it smooth.'

'Oh yes, and black,' she added. 'I want it black.'

Dearest Robert,

Thank you for your two letters which arrived together yesterday though they were weeks old. I am glad you are having a good time and they are making you comfortable in the hotel. It sounds lovely. Alison loved talking to you on the phone on Wednesday. I was across the road at the Fox-Coutts's. Ninni had decided to restart her 'clarss' without telling us and I had to leave the children alone. The Fox-Couttses said it was ridiculous of me to stay in when it was so near and I could even run across and look at them after dinner. It was terribly extravagant of you to ring. Was it just a whim? I suppose it must have been early afternoon for you. I do hope nothing was wrong.

(Does one have whims in the afternoon? Why do I assume things are more likely to go wrong in the afternoon? I am sitting so still that I can hear Ninni's breathing as she comes through the front door. I hate the afternoon. She's been to Biba's and the V & A. She'll be carrying a packet of post cards from the V & A. I can hear her big black boots creaking as she goes up the stairs. In a minute—there!—the slam of the bedroom door. The drawing-room all around me is as clean and light and bright as the picture of a drawing-room. And I am the picture of a woman sitting in it.)

It is very cold here—

(What horrible hyacinths on this writing desk. Maroon. Fat, short, maroon. Is that Robert in that gold frame? Robert Shaw Q.C. the day he took silk. Idiotic when you think of it, a full-bottomed wig. Why do wigs make faces cunning? How I hate those bulbs. Fat wax candles— 'There were feathery green trees—delicate. It was a most lovely afternoon.')

It is very cold here, but no snow. We went to the Round Pond on Saturday. There were not many there. I told you in my last letter about the Taylors. Those friends of your mother were there. The fat ones. The Noddy people. They seemed to think the children—ours —must be grown up! I got my green dress draggled at a petrol place on the way home and had to wear my silver thing at the Fox-Coutts's. That man Henry Something was there and said would I like to go out to a point-to-point so I can't have looked too bad. He said, 'with the children'. Old Judge Fletcher was there, too— I thought he was with you. Apparently he's going out in the vacation. Henry Thing had a driver to take him home—sitting outside in Campden Hill all evening. He must have been terribly cold. But a *white Rolls*!! Lord F. was going back to Wimbledon on the tube. He's a bit of an old duck, isn't he. I'm really rather in love with him.

The children's parties were a success—but I told you

about that. The telegrams came all right. Marmalade
likewise— I've done some tangerine.

(Robert, Robert, Robert!)

Next week I've got tickets for *Peter Pan*—

(Robert!)

It's been going rather a long time but—

(Wait. Listen. Thump! Ninni's boot is coming off.
Thump. Ninni's other boot is coming off. She must be
getting into bed again. Whatever has she been doing
between coming in and taking her boots off? Standing at
the window presumably.

Oh, why ever do I have her. She's no help. But then
there's nothing to help with. There is nothing to do.
Especially in the afternoon.)

Anne put her head down on the desk and said, loud and
clear, 'He is being unfaithful to me.'

'If I look up,' she thought, 'I'll look at my watch and
see that there's ages to go before the school-run. Through
the open door I'll see into the kitchen clean and tidy and
the trolley long ago laid, for tea.'

'Shall I put mine to Daddy in with yours?' asked Andy
that evening, coming in and leaning against her.

'Yes, if you like, dear.'

He leaned harder, touching all of her that he could
and pressing his head into her shoulder. 'Is that all you've
written?'

'I think so this time.'

'It's not much. Mine's a bit short, too.'

'It certainly is,' said Anne.

'Have you said anything about your hair?'

'No, not actually. Have you?'

'Not actually.'

Dear Anne,

Yesterday (Sunday) we went on an expedition into the Blue Mountains. They all have a house there—all being a millionth of a per cent. The very rich. The legal eagles. The feelthy lawyers like us. My word I wish it *were* like this in England—a house for every season. This one was to get away from the heat in August. We went up in two cars after a superb luncheon at somebody's other house—a little bell rung between courses and in comes a maid in cap and apron. It reminded me of your mother and Edinburgh. The hospitality here! It would drive you nearly crazy worrying how to pay back. It does me too rather. Well, we left this house for a sea-side one (number three) and then went up and up from the sea-side to the mountains.

There is not any jungle, which surprised me. All is lush, green forest with unexpected things growing in it haphazard, here and there. Sometimes the country opens out and turns into a brilliant sort of Surrey—then back to forest. Always there are flowers and sudden bright fruit stalls shining with pineapples, etc., under the trees. The children run at you with pots of pink orchids.

The house we visited next was like *Homes and Gardens*, with terraces of English roses (very high in the mountains now) and reminded me of rich Wilts except that the birds were strange—long, high calls—and as dark fell the tremendous clatter and shrieks of the tree creatures. There are fire flies and glow worms like lamps in the bushes. I caught one in my hands. The house had doors and window frames of mahogany and a kitchen of steel and glass, four-poster beds like Heals, fitted carpets, log fires, dreadful pictures. There were great jars full of lilies though only servants are in the house for months together. We sat eating pâté de foie gras and drinking liqueur whisky. Down the hill from the house are people who sleep on the forest floor with four sticks and a little rag or a bit of tin for a roof to keep the rain off. We saw some of them—two or three families coming back from church, all laughing and talking together, the women in hats rather like your Auntie Mary's and all carrying prayer books. Lovely people.

Mrs Santamarina and I (she's the Bolivian Queen) walked a little way in the forest and came to another house some way from our host's which I liked better—like a Canadian log cabin on a little green lawn and all inside seemed plain and simple. Blue lilies on a bank. It would have been your sort of place. Mrs Santamarina was glad to get back to the pâté de foie! On the way down the mountains we called at yet another house. It was pitch black night by now and we had to hold on to each other to feel our way up the drive. No one had visited this house for months but some unseen gent was in the kitchen and after a time came in in a white coat with Red Stripe beer and fresh coconut. This house reminded me rather of Leatherhead—Leatherhead with such a heavy scent of flowers it drove you nearly crazy. Dinner at the Blue Mountain Restaurant—moonlit waterfall beside our table, green lilies, champagne again and filet en croûte.

Love. In great haste for the con. R.

'Hello?'
'Betty?'
'Yes. I think so.'

'How are you?'

'I don't know. Who is it? It's three in the morning.'

'It's Anne.'

'Heavens! Is it Robert?'

'No.'

'You've heard again?'

'He's sent me some—pages.'

'Anne? Hello, Anne? Are you all right? Look, John's just back. D'you want a word with him? Anne—hello? Are you there?'

'He's been taking out the Bolivian Queen.'

'Oh, nonsense.'

'He took her somewhere plain and simple which would have done for me but didn't suit her.'

'You're making that up. Look duck—it's *three in the morning.*'

'I'm not.'

'Anne? Hello? Have we been cut off?'

'Cut off?'

'Anne?'

'Oh Betty, what can I do?'

'Anne.' The phone went silent. Betty dabbed about in the dark with the receiver trying to put it back, and with the other hand beat round for the bedside light. 'It was Anne,' she said to John, 'frantic!'

'Well the foolish woman should have gone out with him,' he said. 'D'you know, I think there's a bit of wildness in Anne.'

'*Wildness!*' said Betty Beech. 'John, she's as pure as a lily.'

'I didn't say she wasn't pure,' he said, 'but there's a bit of, well—wildness somewhere. I always remember the way she flung her arms about at the wedding.'

Betty had found the light switch and sat up in bed,

looking down at her bronzed and wakeful husband (he was only five hours home. For him it was still early evening). Her own face was shamelessly in a paste. She said, 'Well, it's taking a long time to show. The wedding was about twenty years ago. She's nearly forty. That house! Those children! Robert's shirts! I don't suppose she's forgotten the laundry van in fifteen years. Haven't you noticed his shirts? I wouldn't be surprised if she did them herself, they're so good. And those clever children. She goes through all their homework.'

'That's what I mean. It's not natural. All that energy and —life—wasn't meant for shirts and homework.'

'She's certainly in an odd mood.' Betty sank down and fiddled with the light switch again. 'She rang up the other afternoon—I was asleep then as a matter of fact—and all there was was—well, deep breathing and long silences. I mean—*teenage*! I thought she was just lonely. She said, "What shall I do?" I thought she meant there was some crisis on and I was thinking I'd have to go round though of course it's miles from Chelsea—but it turned out she actually *meant* it. Just *that*! She had nothing to do! It made me feel—d'you know it made me feel almost frightened. It was horrible. I said, "Go to the Tate," and d'you know what she said?—"Why?" '

'Yes,' he said, 'there's something latent about Anne.'

'*Latent*? Anne? I wouldn't have said there was a latent thing in her. She just looks straight at you all the time.'

'I expect Cleopatra looked straight at you all the time.'

'Well, Cleopatra wasn't latent. She was all rolling and surging out from the very start. On permanent exhibition. Anne—'

'I wonder,' said John, 'what Anne will put on exhibition in the end. She'll have to, in the end you know. Otherwise—'

'Otherwise?'

'Otherwise,' he said, 'she'll crack up.'

'What was Robert up to out there anyway?' Betty wriggled down in the charcoal-coloured sheets.

'Robert?' John began to laugh, 'good old Robert,' he said and laughed a bit more.

'Well, what? Womanising?'

'Oh, I wouldn't say—'

She put out the light and yawned and turned away from him. 'Men,' she said. 'They never give a thing away.'

'Robert's a very amusing fellow, you know,' said John still laughing at something. 'Irresistible to a certain type of woman I'd say, wouldn't you?'

'Not to me,' said Betty, 'he's got glittery eyes. He watches you. He goes round playing enigmas!'

'I suppose I'm not an enigma.' He was still snorting now and then—very wide awake—about Robert Shaw.

'As a dinner plate,' said his wife, 'and don't blow down my neck.'

In the morning John said they must have Anne round to dinner, with the Taylors, perhaps, and that chap Henry Doings.

Dear Daddy,

Thank you for the lovely post card of the Botanical Gardens which look very nice. We have three new girls at school this term and two new teachers who are super especially the Latin and Mummy is not having to help me at all. Also we have swimming now twice a week and are beginning lacrosse which is a most peculiar game founded by the Red Indians and involves standing very still for long periods of time in the cold or alternatively being massacred. My friend and I are thinking of getting up a petition about it on account of the danger. It is very good for posture.

Sorry for a short letter. It is a note to go in with Mummy's. There is a dustbin strike here and it is very cold. Mummy is a bit vague these days and I think you will be surprised to see her HAIR. ***Come back soon. I miss you and I love you, Alison.

P.S. See*** above. I MEAN IT. See it. PLEASE.

Holding this letter in an envelope big enough to take her letter too, but still unsealed, Anne sat on a public seat in the immense forecourt of the Natural History Museum.

It was a week later. Her head was tilted back, her eyes were closed and her long legs stuck out before her in boots nearly as long, expensive boots but sombre. She was quite alone there, for it was a weekday and bitterly cold, Kensington blowy and dead, not a glimmer of light in a tired white sky.

Behind her closed eyes a long, quiet wave uncoiled itself along a sandy shore. Like the Kensington sky the wave was white, but it existed against a dazzle of blue, or blue-black moonlit sea. Robert sat, or rather reclined upon a long chair on a pale beach and beside him on another, her perfect profile raised proudly to the night, reclined the Bolivian Queen.

The long, white wave died and after a minute another began effortlessly to unfold itself, the marble patterns on its arched back clearly to be seen in the astonishing light of the moon.

The night was hot. Hot. The Bolivian Queen's arm slept like a plump gold snake along the arm of her chair and not two inches away lay Robert's arm. Music from the hotel above the beach could be softly heard though palms concealed all lights save that of the moon and stars.

Robert's hand rose like the wave and moved to cover the hand of the Boliv—

Anne sat up. She took Alison's letter out of the envelope, tore it to little bits and watched the birds who sit always invisible on the cliff tops of the Museum swoop to eat them. They strutted quarrelsomely about, complaining and looking foolish before flying back. She took out her own letter, tore and scattered it. Then the envelope, tore and scattered it. Fewer birds flew down this time but those that did were equally bad-tempered. They twittered and fussed and watched acutely. She said, 'Poor things,' and gave them a biscuit from her bag. Immediately, from the small movement of her hand came thousands of birds, swooping in from far away. 'What eyes they have,' she thought. There were hundreds and hundreds of birds now, about her feet, crowding the seat, on her very arms, her shoulders, her knees. 'It's like when Allie was a baby,' she thought. 'I'd forgotten it.' She laughed and sang to them,

> Allie, call the birds in,
> The birds from the sky !
> Allie calls, Allie sings,
> Down they all fly.

'Ages and ages ago,' she said out loud. 'Robert had hardly any work. We had such fun. Allie in her push-chair. We were so happy. It all made such sense.'

She held her arms out to the birds and found to her surprise that her eyes had spilled over with tears. Also that the jowly man from the Fox-Coutts's was standing observing her through the railings.

She stood up in the cloud of birds as he paced away slowly down the road, then through the gigantic gates and

D

up the asphalt slope of the great drive and back towards her. 'I thought it was you,' he said gravely and drawing off a glove took her hand like an old family doctor. 'I thought it was you.'

When he let go of her hand he put the glove back on again. It was a fine glove of soft, chestnut leather with tiny little pricks all over it in threes. It was a plump glove like a clutch of cigars. He himself was heavy rather than plump—in a large black overcoat very thick and soft, and a bowler hat. Between hat and coat his face hung in folds of the greatest moment.

'There is some difference . . .' he said.

'Yes. Oh yes, Just a sort of rinse.'

'No children today?' he said looking round as though they might be lined up somewhere.

'No. They're all going out to tea in various directions.' (He must be sixty.) 'They've been getting a lot of invitations lately. With their father away—'

'Which must leave you—'

'Oh, I've been getting a lot of invitations, too.' (Well, fifty-five.)

They were pacing together now along the path, back to the gates and along the pavement. Just around the corner in Exhibition Road, Anne saw the white Rolls flagrantly parked, the driver to attention in grey beside it, stiff as an ornament.

'Invitations,' she thought, 'invitations of a kind. A nice quiet, solemn kind. The kind you're going to hand out in a minute.'

'We must arrange that point-to-point,' he said. 'Let me take you somewhere now. Were you going back towards Campden Hill?'

He bent forward. Quite sixty.

But what about me? A minute ago I was talking to

birds. I was singing to the birds like a mad old woman. I might be sixty. What difference is there between me and sixty? Did I say that out loud?

'. . . for tea?'

Presumably not.

'What? Sorry. No thanks.' But she couldn't go another step. Down in the soft leather of the car the large, dark overcoat was very close and they slid like cream up Exhibition Road, round the corner, past Kensington Palace Road, past the Hypermarket and up to dear old Barkers. At the lights at the beginning of Kensington High Street the car had to stop and four fat cigars and a thumb fastened gently round her upper arm.

Anne was out of the Rolls and away up Church Street on her long boots with Henry Whatsname puffing behind.

'Somewhere for tea!'

'No thanks.'

'I do beg your pardon. There's a nice place in—'

'No thanks. No. I'm walking. I like walking. It does me good. I walk a lot.'

'Let me walk with you.'

'It's a long way,' she said, still striding out. 'Church Street's quite steep. You don't notice it in a car.'

But he kept pace rather well.

She went faster. By the time she was at the end of Sheffield Terrace she was nearly running. She turned. He was still there, and, turning again at the top of Peel Street before crossing the road, she found that she was utterly incensed to see that the Rolls was still there, too, easing itself round the parked cars in the narrow road full of pseudo cottages, in silent bottom gear.

'The car's still with us!' She hadn't the least idea why she was so angry. She almost stamped her foot. She did stamp her foot.

Henry turned to regard the scene. There could be no denial. 'I keep the car about,' he said apologetically.

'I saw that once in a film,' she snarled and flew towards Campden Hill Square, along Aubrey Walk, and behind her Henry Thing stepped out manfully and the Rolls came smoothly on. And at her front door as she searched frantically in all her pockets for keys, Henry was beside her still, though mopping his face. He had removed the hat.

'Might I ask . . .'

'Oh, for goodness sake *ask*,' she said, 'I hate it, that's all. The film I saw it was lovely, that's all.' She flung off her coat and let it fall to the floor.

'It was romantic. It was about love. It was Mercouri. I'll bet you've never even heard of Mercouri, have you? They were walking along—he was terribly young—by the Thames or the Seine or something. She threw a ring in the river—a huge great emerald or something. So what about that? And there was a great big car creeping along behind them. But it was *different*. Oh, take your silly coat and those awful gloves off.'

She flew into the kitchen and seized the silver tea-pot. It gleamed as she took it out of its baize bag. It suggested moonlight. She rushed into the drawing-room.

'D'you know something? I want to look like Mercouri. As a matter of fact I do. I do look like her. Look when I scrape my hair back—what's left of it. I was born in Edinburgh. I was very well brought up. I got distinction in Domestic Science and I can translate Latin. I've plenty of money and lovely children and my husband is faithful to me. There now. I know he is. So. Even in Jamaica with a Bolivian Queen who burns on the water.'

'But I'm like Mercouri,' she cried, 'and I'm dead sick of Kensington and children and point-to-points and *order*. I'm sick of *order*,' she shrieked at the departing hippopotamus back of Henry Thing. Bellowing from the doorstep, listening to herself with interest, she watched it and the rest of him being driven hastily away.

Then she ran back into the house. Ninni hung over the stairs like a black cloud. She ran into the drawing-room, the hall, the kitchen gathering up the remains of the maroon hyacinths, the *Liberal News*, anything in her path she could carry. She tore down the pegboard and tickets, green-shield stamps, time-tables. Free offers flew about like leaves, pound notes (Oh Edinburgh!) floated away. She seized *The Times*, the Parish Magazine, Alison's Latin books from the hall table. She ran back into the front garden and among the bay trees and the chain she burned the lot.

She raised her head and cried, 'There,' watched by Ninni from a top window and not a few people from across the street.

Betty Beech, coming back from despatching little boxes of wedding cake with Mrs Fox-Coutts, flew to the telephone and John ('*Black* hair, darling! Flames!'). And Ninni opened the window.

Ninni called sorrowfully to her, 'Come.'

'What, Ninni?' Anne laughed.

'Come, Mrs Shaw. It is the phone. It is Jamaica for you.'

'All right,' Anne cried, 'all right, Ninni dear. Tell him I'm coming. I'm coming right away.'

9   *Something to Tell the Girls*

Imagine a nonsense.

Imagine in *The Times* newspaper—perhaps the Personal Column—the following item:

> 'Miss Dee-Dee and Miss Gongers of Harrogate Hall, at present holidaying in the West Indies, today hired a motor car in the outskirts of Kingston, Jamaica, and set out on an expedition to the Blue Mountains.'

Imagine this. Suspend disbelief. Consider, as jaws revolve on toast, and bacon is eased from molars, as cornflakes crunch in several continents, this item being read. And imagine then a symphony of feminine shrieks, the scraping back of chairs, the rush of feet to telephones and the following conversation taking place, identical in several parts of the turning earth.

'They *can't* still be teaching!'

'They can't still be *alive*!'

'They certainly can't still be *driving*? Did they ever?'

'If they are it certainly won't be for long. I suppose it'll be Gongers?'

'Well it certainly won't be Dee-Dee.'

Shrieks and laughs.

And shrieks and laughs of not one generation only, for Miss Dee-Dee and Miss Gongers had been at Harrogate Hall (Junior French, Senior History) since before the flood.

Since before the War anyway. Not one but half a dozen
eras of girls had said, 'Since before the War', about
Miss Dee-Dee and Miss Gongers, meaning quite different
wars. They dressed—they had always dressed, the two
of them—in a style suggesting even before the Boer War,
though that of course, could certainly not be so. Could
it?

Miss Dee-Dee and Miss Gongers were among the first
batch of not very young young ladies to be allowed to go
to Cambridge. They had met there, chaperoned by the
mutual friend of an aunt. They had left Cambridge—
chins held high under Leghorn straws—with the precious
piece of paper—not of course a degree—to say that they
had completed the course and satisfied the examiners. And
they had left unencumbered by romance for they were
stern days those and work was hard. Also it was important
to try and pass out higher than the men. Miss Gongers was
a shining example of this sternness and labour and spoke
widely of the resultant glory to her sex of its full academic
fruition now. Miss Dee-Dee of course agreed, though she
was a pastel, gentle person and there had been a young
man and a soft spring day in the Fellows' Garden . . . In
the end however romance passed her by.

Nor did romance show itself much at Harrogate where
the two young women proceeded, Miss Dee-Dee in a
muslin dress and a brim of roses, Miss Gongers in more
militant attire. It was Harrogate Hall for the Daughters of
Gentlemen—believe it or believe it not—and they set
about teaching with the same devotion and conviction
that ever Florence Nightingale proclaimed at Scutari some
time—well not all that long—before. They would have
been quite at home with Miss Nightingale, both of them.
Or anyway, Miss Gongers would.

They had taught grandmothers. Young grandmothers

certainly, but grandmothers. More granddaughters wrote to grandmothers each year.

'Dear Granny,' they wrote,

Yes—Miss Dee-Dee and Miss Gongers *are* still here! Miss Dee-Dee's sweet. Wouldn't hurt a fly. She teaches the first years. She has a pink face and blue eyes and reads the new ones Beatrix Potters. We're far too old for Beatrix Potters but she still reads them. She's got terribly old editions—I expect *first* editions and our dormi head says if you're homesick you go and see Miss Dee-Dee and she'll give you Harrogate toffee and Mrs Tiggy Winkle. Actually she is absolutely exactly *like* Mrs Tiggy Winkle. She sends her love and says do you still get hay fever!!! Miss Gongers came up to me the first day and said, '*Elspeth's* granddaughter, I think. I hope you'll be better at dates.' She's *terrifying*. Like a sort of iron giraffe. I must say she's a bit of a prize, though. She wears long crêpe dresses—marvellous—and gold glasses, but someone said she does still go out sometimes and takes hockey!!!! In knee socks!!!!! Oh, do come down and see them. And me. And thanks a million for the mun and records. Better not let D & G see those though. Buckets of love, Caroline. P.S. No, our letters don't get censored now.

And so on.

Miss Dee-Dee and Miss Gongers like the love of God stretched out from generation unto generation and such an item in *The Times* might have been read as widely and enthusiastically as anything else in it.

'But, Gongers,' said Miss Dee-Dee timidly as a great lorry whirled by in a cloud of dust.

Gongers did not speak. A bus called 'Sing to Jesus'

squealed past on the crown of the road, its driver leaning out sideways pumping up and down a great black forearm.

'Gongers, I think—'

'Did you hear what he said?'

'No, but—'

A tremendous howling and screeching and two cars kindly opened before them, passing on either side.

'Gongers, I believe it is the *left*-hand side.'

'Nonsense,' said Gongers. She proceeded on the right. They were on a quieter piece of road now, curving and climbing. 'They changed to the right when they threw us out. Naturally one respects their laws, however mistaken.'

Nevertheless, after a minute she changed to the left. The car laboured its way into the foothills of the forest.

'Do you know,' said Dee-Dee, 'do you know, Gongs, I had no idea that you could drive a motor.'

Miss Gongers's ancient Nefertiti neck strained forward as she kept her eyes upon the road. Her expression signified that she found this not extraordinary.

'I mean—the licence?'

'I have always possessed a licence.'

'But isn't there some—test one takes?'

'I never took a test.'

A disintegrating Rolls-Royce filled with two Jamaican families en vacances or en fête and also believing that since the fall of the Raj Jamaica drove on the right, shot past them with a terrible blast of wind.

'I never took a test,' said Miss Gongers, '(See, dear, where the river has taken away the verge.) I never took a test because my first licence was obtained before tests were invented. It was while you were in Schleswig I expect— that summer, just before the War. All through the War— the next War—oh' (The car fell a foot on to an unexpected lower level.) 'All through the War I paid five shillings a

D*

year in order to preclude the necessity of taking a test at the end of it.'

'But you have never driven *since* then, dear, have you?'

'No—a bicycle is healthier in Harrogate. In the holidays there have been motor-coach tours. Well, you know there have.

'Anyway,' she added, narrowly missing a mongoose and swinging out towards the carpet of forest tree tops that bordered the outside edge of the hair-pin bend, 'I am not keen on driving in England now. It is unsafe . . . My word, Deeds,' she said in a minute and with a sudden spark, 'I'm glad we did it. We're climbing now all right. We'd never have got here without a car of our own. It's miles from a bus route.'

A man came out from the trees ahead of them and glared. Miss Gongers tooted at him. He spat.

'I hope we are wise,' Miss Dee-Dee said. 'I hope we don't meet trouble.'

'Wise?' said Gongers, 'you didn't want to spend the rest of the time on those wretched hot package beaches did you? Or in one of those private taxis going off to look at baskets in markets? And the organised tours are prohibitive.'

'Look out!' cried Dee-Dee. But it was only a group of children and their mothers, darting out at them from under the trees, their arms held out before them like sticks, holding pots of orchids.

'Orchids!' Miss Dee-Dee gasped.

'No good,' pronounced Gongers, taking a corner, on one wheel, 'we'd never get them home. Will you shut the windows?'

Dee-Dee wound up windows. One refused to wind. As she struggled with it she realised that she was experiencing an odd yet reminiscent sensation. 'Why, Gongers,' she said, 'it's getting quite cold.' She looked around her at the trees, they were not palm trees any more. They had damp trunks. They were ferny. They dripped with cold-looking water. Jamaica! 'And, goodness! It's getting foggy!'

'Aha,' said Gongers, speeding on.

In Newcastle they stopped and got out. 'Perhaps we ought to leave the engine running,' said Dee-Dee, but Miss Gongers put her mind to it and remembered the formula for switching off. 'Nonsense,' she said, 'they showed me the start at the motor hire. Perfectly simple. I can't think why they seemed so nervous. It has all come back to me perfectly and, what is more, I *like* the four gears. They are stimulating. Come along, let's get out and walk about.'

On the wide terrace, the great parade ground of New-castle where British soldiers had marched for so many years, the old ladies paced about. People began to gather in knots, the women with their arms folded and grinning under pink cotton head-gear. More children with orchids sidled up, automatically drifting towards Miss Dee-Dee, who as automatically spread out her arms.

'My dears,' she said, 'Orchids! But you see we wouldn't be allowed to take them home. Back to England, you see.'

'You from England then, ma'am?'

'Yes, dear. From Harrogate, in England. Not far from another place called Newcastle.'

'You don't have no orchids there, ma'am?'

'Not like these, dear.'

'Harrogate has got *beautiful* flowers,' Miss Gongers broke in resonantly. 'And very beautiful Valley Gardens.'

'Oh, *look* at these orchids!' Dee-Dee begged, holding out small old hands.

'White face, white face,' a boy yelled, 'go home.' But his sister hit him.

'You like Jamaica, ma'am,' asked a lady in a nasturtium-coloured dress, standing with tilted hip.

'Oh, we *love* Jamaica.'

'The British,' announced Gongers, standing tall as the Duke of Wellington, 'have always loved Jamaica.' Pointing up at the high rock wall above her with the huge plaques of ancient regiments she said, 'My father was a member of that regiment and my grandfather before him.'

The Jamaicans were lost for a reply—then a little girl began to giggle, and a man standing at a little distance, propped against the iron railings, laughed. A breath of ill wind blew across the terrace.

'Hush,' said Miss Dee-Dee.

'You go home. Go home and call us Jamaican monkeys, hey?' a voice shouted.

'Hush! Good gracious!' Miss Dee-Dee exclaimed. She patted a woolly head and followed Miss Gongers back to the car. 'Back, I think,' she said, much flustered. 'Such nice people— Whatever did we do? How very horrible.'

'Back?' said Gongers, 'oh, come. We must go on.' With concentration she started the engine and moved forward with a rush, scattering the orchid bearers. 'Aha,' she said, and swept across the square, out of the high town and away off into the higher mountains.

The road was rough now and narrower, quite different from the way they had already travelled. It was more twisting and lonelier. The crags of the mountains were masked with pines—pines living in such a damp and sunless air that they had grown grey fur coats that hung in tattered rags, thick, ancient cobwebs that trailed the ground. There was not a flower beneath them, not a gleam of light.

'We're in the clouds,' said Dee-Dee.

'Proving that being in the clouds is not what it is

thought to be,' said Gongers. 'It's something one might tell the girls.'

However, they swung soon out of the darkest part, over a splashing stream that crossed the road to where the air was clear. Pine woods rose rank on rank, almost black against a rainy sky to the very tops of the immense heights of the mountains. 'A mixture of the Tyrol,' said Miss Gongers, 'and Leatherhead.' They swooped upwards on a stony track and another swoop opened to the left. Miss Gongers put her pointed shoe down hard on the accelerator for this second swoop, swung magnificently round it and embedded the radiator and front bumper high up into a bank of giant blue lilies.

The engine stopped and silence fell over the mountains.

'Yes,' said Gongers, as if this was just what she had expected. 'Yes, yes, yes.' She switched off the engine, which in any case had stopped, and they both got out. The cloud, that had obligingly drifted away, now drifted back again, obscuring everything. Standing in the road in their cotton dresses the two old ladies shivered. 'Did you bring a cardigan, Deeds?' Miss Gongers was walking round the car and bending to look beneath it from various angles.

'No, dear. After all we've been so terribly hot—I never thought . . .'

'Ah well.' Miss Gongers straightened up. 'We came because they said it was cool in the mountains and cool we are.'

'Cool we are,' said Miss Dee-Dee unsurely. Shivering. 'You did put all the brakes on, dear? It does seem to be rather at a—tilt.'

'Of course,' said Gongers. The car in fact seemed to be almost vertical, belly to belly with the bank, desperate, like a climber surprised.

'There is something odd about the back wheel too,

don't you think? The tyre seems to be flat. I think we'll have to walk, dear.'

'Down to Newcastle? Oh Gongers, it's miles!'

'We might go on a little upwards perhaps. There might be a village or a police post or something. After all we must be nearly at the top of the pass.'

'I don't see that that—' Miss Dee-Dee's voice had risen though, being Miss Dee-Dee's, it was not of course querulous.

'Why not?' Gongers asked sharply. 'There's always *something* at the top of a pass. Look at Switzerland.'

'But it's not Switzerland,' said Dee-Dee wishing profoundly that it were.

And her wish was answered for round the corner of the road the mists swam away again for a moment and a small Swiss chalet was astoundingly revealed, made of pine trunks, with pointed gables and check curtains at the windows. It stood on a little green alp all by itself surveying the clouds and the tree tops. It had a small stone terrace with an iron seat and round the door someone had planted beds of flowers. There was a child's teddy bear sitting on the terrace, very soggy. Otherwise there was no sign of life.

'Well, bless my soul. Dear Gongers, bless my soul!'

'There you are,' said Gongers triumphantly, 'now this is convenient,' and she marched over the lawn with Dee-Dee behind her and they knocked on the door.

Then they walked about and looked in the windows (rather untidy) and called a time or two, but nobody answered. There was a padlock properly fastened on the door and the windows were well barred.

'They can't be far though,' said Dee-Dee, thinking of the bear. 'There's washing-up to be done. Someone's been here very recently. If we wait about—'

'I thought I heard someone,' said Gongers and they stood quite still. But there was only the long clear pipe of the solitaires in the forest.

'Solitaires,' said Dee-Dee, 'oh, those must be the solitaires. Some people live in Jamaica all their lives and never hear the solitaires.'

Gongers, on steely tiptoe, made her way all round the chalet once again. 'There is no one,' she said, 'yet I'm sure I heard . . . It is a holiday house. Deeds, there may be nobody here for weeks!' The clouds swept slowly back, blotting out the view again and muffling the bird song. They stood looking at each other on the cold and now invisible lawn. 'I am afraid that we are quite alone,' said Miss Gongers in a voice that faced facts.

But back at the car she was proved wrong, for standing beside it quite silently were two men. Miss Gongers whose mind had been put to the test the past minutes quickly shut her eyes and opened them again. 'Er—Deeds— Do you see?'

Dee-Dee joined her at the lily bank. 'Oh—*people*. Well! You were *right*. You *did* hear people! Oh what a blessing!'

'HellO!' Gongers called in hockey match tones and strode off to the road with Dee-Dee behind, 'How absolutely splendid. How *really* splendid. I cannot tell you how delighted we are to see you. We have really been very— How do you do?'

The two men had yellow whites to their eyes and were chewing something. They did not speak.

'Let me introduce—' said Gongers. 'I am Miss Gongham. This is my friend Miss Deeds. We are from England. This is our car.' She held out her hand and after a pause one of the men slowly took it, first moving his gun into

his left hand. The other man turned away and gave the
car wheel a kick.

'Yes,' said Gongers, 'yes, I know. I'm afraid it is a puncture on top of everything else. But if perhaps you could
just get the car off the bank. Just a good heave. A *good*
heave, perhaps—oh dear! Is that thunder?'

Neither of the men spoke but the one who had kicked the
car kicked it again.

'Oh, I say,' said Gongers, 'I shouldn't do that. It will do
no good whatsoever. Now just stay where you are and I
will lean in and release the brake. Then both of you give
a pull. Dee-Dee dear, just take the guns.'

Miss Gongers dived into the car and dealt with the
hand-brake. Miss Dee-Dee, smiled at the men and collected
in the guns as though they had been exercise books. After
an initial small shove by Miss Gongers the men quickly
got out of the car's path and assisted it into an horizontal
position.

'Now—the jack. Dee-Dee, put the guns in the car. They
will get rusty.' It was raining hard now and thunder
seemed very close at hand. 'Come along, Dee-Dee dear,
you get in too. These kind friends will get the jack from
the boot, I'm sure.'

Waiting until she saw them very slowly, and almost in
a trance, begin to open up the boot, she herself got behind
the wheel. Mutterings were heard without and the face of
one of the men—his eyes were very strange and dead, his
mouth not happy—appeared at the window. He said something in a hoarse voice. There was a strong, odd smell
about him. He had gingerish crinkly hair, an orange skin
and a chain round his neck. He seemed to be suggesting
that they get out of the car again.

'We are making it too heavy,' said Dee-Dee and
removed her tiny bird-like frame from the passenger seat.

Gongers followed. 'Very well,' she said, 'do let's get a move on though, shall we?'

The second man, the kicker, swung the jack heavily about in his hands.

'Shall we?' Gongers gleamed over her arched nose. In the voice were forty-seven years of hockey, of supervision of the cross-country, of fixing in the mind the clauses of the Treaty of Amiens, of pressing home the iniquity of reading by torch beneath blankets, of . . .

The jack was placed and vigorously set to work and the back, left-hand corner of the car slowly rose into the air. The wheel however stayed upon the ground.

Even the two gunmen were surprised and the first one, the one who had shaken hands, met Miss Dee-Dee's eyes and gave a sudden huge crow of laughter. At almost the same moment there was a rending, blazing flash up behind them by the house and a crash of thunder like Armageddon. Gunmen and ladies leapt for the car with a composite leap and sat there rigid as the rain cracked down.

'Mind the guns,' said Miss Gongers, 'don't trample them on the floor. I am afraid of guns. I believe that they should be forbidden. I do not believe in shooting of any kind on any pretext whatsoever. I only hope,' she said glaring sternly at the wet men through the driving mirror, 'that you were not shooting solitaires.'

And half an hour later they still sat there stiffly.

The storm had turned the road into a stony brown river, thunder boomed and rattled above and the rain poured down. To assist things one of the men took off his jacket and fixed it over the window which did not wind up. He muttered to his friend now and then. They took out a bottle from a pocket and a strong smell of rum invaded the car.

'I suppose we ought to play a game or something,' said Miss Gongers.

'Or tell stories,' said Miss Dee-Dee.

The men had no views on this, but Miss Dee-Dee felt very tempted. *'The Tailor of Gloucester?'* she said. 'It is very adult.' But Miss Gongers thought not. Looking in the mirror again, she suggested a song. 'Shall we sing?' she asked, and as nothing resulted but rather heavier breathing struck up 'The Ash Grove'; and after a nervous false start Miss Dee-Dee joined in. The gunmen jumped out of the car and disappeared into the forest.

'Really,' said Miss Gongers, 'they are so very extraordinary. It makes me feel one will never understand them. Such good Christians too. Every denomination so well represented. I do like them all so much. Oh dear—we never even gave them a tip.'

A second nonsense :
The Times. April—197–
Personal.

A multiple puncture belonging to Miss Dee-Dee and Miss Gongers of Harrogate Hall was repaired late last evening by a policeman at a police box two miles down the mountain on which it occurred in the Jamaican rain forests. The ladies had rolled the two miles to the post on the car wheel's rim which Miss Gongers had cleverly and with Divine assistance freed from a faulty jack. As the clattering vehicle approached the police box, the officer was seen to buckle on his gun belt, but took it off again on examination of the passengers. He took them into his cement shed, made them tea on a calor gas ring, tried the jack, flung it into the forest and loosed the wheel by the process of lifting the whole motor car up in his two hands. He then found the ladies blankets, coconut, and bread and accommodated them for the night—one in his bunk and the other on two chairs. He himself slept in the empty prison cell. In the morning he saw them off with the recommendation that they stop for nobody, adding that this was advice. Miss Gongers gave him her well-known handshake while Miss Dee-Dee took one of his hands in both her own and nearly kissed it.

'Trained by us of course,' said Gongers whirling down the mountain, 'the real old English policeman. A magnificent man. A very moving episode.'

'Yes,' said Miss Deeds. She was a little stiff this morning. 'It will be nice to have a bath and a proper rest though, and feel that it is over.'

'But it was a great experience,' said Gongers, 'and something to tell the girls.'

They had reached Kingston now and in the rush hour traffic Gongers was driving slowly in the slow lane. 'After all,' she said, 'this sort of experience is exactly what we came away from Europe for. A thrilling chapter. I'm almost sad that it is completed.'

And the car stopped.

They were crossing a bridge over some sort of underpass and the maniac traffic was hurtling by. It was the lunch-time rush hour, and the car baked and pulsated in the noon-day sun. Miss Gongers, after trying many things with fingers and toes, sat back and closed her eyes. 'I spoke too soon,' she said and let her hands drop into her lap. Her nose suddenly looked sharp and pale. 'What on earth can be the matter now?' she said and her voice had a most unfamiliar high and wavering quality.

'Now, don't worry,' said Dee-Dee at once, 'goodness, we're nearly home. You've done wonderfully, Gongers. Now I'll just get out and tell someone. It'll be no time at all.' She was quickly back at the window. 'Dear,' she said, 'I've found someone. They'll come and get us at once. Now *don't worry*. A nice man in a van. Didn't you see him stop? I don't quite know where he's gone but . . . There. Now, we'll just sit a little. I wonder if it might be cooler out of the car. Shall we go and sit under the bridge down there? It might be in the shade.'

They got out and looked over the parapet. It did not look inviting . The underpass was not so much a road as— well, it might almost have been a great, dry drain (which it was) beating with heat and full of cracks. In one place someone had started a sort of allotment in the dust. There were some desperate looking tomatoes. Near them two black and white vultures were eating a dead dog. 'I don't think it looks cooler down there,' said Gongers.

'Perhaps under the bridge,' said Dee-Dee. They picked their way, tottering a little, down the steep ramp of the drain and sat upon a cement block inside the central pier, but it was, as Miss Gongers had thought, much hotter. It smelled quite dreadfully and beneath the bridge was unspeakable filth. 'This will not do,' said Gongers, 'we must go back.' But they sat on under the pitiless sun quite unable to move.

And presently the children began to appear all round them, popping up from cracks and crannies, sliding out of the tin shacks that grew like sores along the banks of the drain. They were thin children—very thin about the legs and some of them were ugly and dressed in bits of rag. They stood round the old ladies in a circle and one or two began to call things out.

Soon they all began to call things out and when they found they were not answered they began to push forward and several started to do a sort of derisive dance. They came in closer. They clustered round.

'Children,' said Miss Gongers, 'not like the pretty ones up in the mountains.'

'Poor little dears,' was all Miss Dee-Dee could say.

The children began to laugh and shout and push, to come in close, to argue who should get nearest and feel brooches and bags and hats. A stone flew and someone began to cry. At the second stone Miss Gongers gave herself a great shake and stood up. Summoning all her powers she walked forward taking first one child by the hand and then a second. The others squealed and pressed forward but she still walked on, right into the middle of the drain and then stood still. 'Now,' she said.

'White face,' screamed a child.

'Dee-Dee, will you see to that one. He's so little. And take the other young ones will you? That's right.' Miss Dee-Dee with a sigh also stood up. Then clapped her hands.

'The little ones to Miss Deeds and the big ones to me,' called Miss Gongers. 'Two lines please. Now—who's to be leader? That's right. No fighting now. Straight lines, then off we go. Who knows "Oranges and Lemons?"'

'Sit now and be quiet,' said Miss Dee-Dee, 'quite, quite quiet—' Her voice died to a whisper and all the children's voices ceased, 'Once upon a time there was an old cat, called Mrs Tabitha Twitchit . . .'

'Oh very nice, very nice,' came Miss Gongers's voice as the lines took shape, 'and *lovely* singing. I wish my girls at home could see this dancing. My word. Now who can sing "Here we go gathering . . ."? That's the way. Now off you go.'

The rabble of children turned to dancers, skinny legs pranced, white teeth gleamed. A sort of song began to rise. First one line wavered forward, then the other to meet it, "Here we come gathering . . ."

'You have the idea,' Miss Gongers cried.

It was Mrs Ingham who saw them. She was accompanying Miranda on the school run and a traffic jam on the bridge had caused Miranda to remark in passing or rather in sticking, that the bridge spanned a huge dry drain built against the hurricane floods but used in fact to grow tomatoes. Mrs Ingham nipped out of the car at once and jutted her chin over the parapet where she viewed the dead dog.

'Tomatoes,' she said, 'need *regular* fertiliser.'

Then, surveying a whirling group and a static group of children and two fragile scarecrows who appeared in some uncanny way to be in charge of them, she cried, 'Miranda! Come here. Quickly. It *can't* be!' and Miranda, heaving herself alongside said, 'Good Lord, it is!'

And so the two old things were rescued and lived to tell the tale.

In years to come anthropologists were to be interested and flummoxed by a legend of singing priestesses in a motor car in the mountains and by a localised calypso in the plain about roly-poly puddings and rats, executions, and the churches of London, hawthorn, frost and citrus fruits and candles that light you to bed.

10　*Monique*

'No, not that way, darling.'

Ned was steered away. He tripped and upset someone in a long evening dress. He lay on the dance floor under the warm night sky, kicked with his toes and wept.

It was a bad, a troubled evening at Pineapple Bay. People were uneasy in the heavy air, for April was nearly over and the smart days were done. Soon would come the conventions, the package tours. No more the scarce-overheard murmurings on the beach at the next distant beach table, 'Yes. I do have one Gauguin.' Next month, maybe next week, the screams of the package wives getting to know each other in the accents of Milwaukee, their husbands sitting in one of the private sitting-rooms, ankle over knee, discussing sales as the tape-recorder wound its quiet coil. 'Well, look at it this way then, Dave . . .'

The little, perfect beach was already receiving less attention from the beach-raker. Deep tunnels of crabs crossed it and made it grey, almost rubbishy by evening. The umbrellas over the white tables were not opened nor dusted down and the waiters carried the club sandwiches just a trifle less high on the shoulder at luncheon time. The season was nearly done.

Yet, 'No. Not that way, Ned darling.'

'Why not? I want to go on the beach.'

'Nobody's allowed on the beach after dark. Never. Look at the notice. You know that.'

There was a notice at the top of the beach steps and also on a sort of blackboard in the green marble foyer. It was there all year—fashion time and package time. NO GUEST IS PERMITTED ON THE BEACH AFTER DARK.

But something or other was going on on the beach tonight.

'Can't I have a look?'

'No, Ned.'

'What's happening?'

'I don't know, Ned.'

'Mummy, why can't we go on the beach after dark?'

'I don't know, darling.'

'Is it ghosts?'

'No. Of course not.'

'Is it gangsters?'

'No. Of course not.'

'Why are there guards then? Later there are.'

'Well, it's nice to have guards. There are guards in London. There are night-watchmen at all the road-works everywhere in the world for instance. Haven't you seen them? They make tea in little stoves, to guard the picks and shovels.'

'There are no picks and shovels on this beach. Mum, what is happening on the beach?'

The band struck up. The singers asked Liza to come back, come back, girl, and reported that they wanted no cream in their coffee. The guests, still the well-dressed ones but not flamboyant, relaxed a little and smiled about them—Lady Fletcher and the judge, a Jamaican judge they were entertaining, Ned and his parents, an American priest, the quiet tourists of the April Indian summer. The warm, sweet, heavy evening wore on. But restlessly a little.

And something certainly was going on on the beach—
something of a kind so difficult and disturbing that the
manager of Pineapple Bay's creamy brow was creased and
the waiters whispered in corners. In the end the owner
of the hotel his very self was called upon the telephone.

'There's trouble here, sir.'

'What sort? Police trouble?'

'No, sir. Queer trouble. We've got a woman on the
beach.'

'A *woman*? From the hotel?'

'Yessir.'

'Well, get her off it, man. It's ten o'clock at night.'

'We can't, sir. She's been there all day. She's not
moving.'

'Have you tried to move her?'

'She just lies there, sir. She's not moving one eye-lash,
sir. She's been there since early morning.'

'American?'

'No. She's a Bolivian. Big stuff, sir.'

'Big stuff?'

'She's a beauty, sir. Husband's gone on to Rio.'

'Ha. Drugs?'

'I don't think so, sir.'

'Drunk?'

'Not at all, sir.'

'Dead?'

'No, sir. She's breathing. But she's just lying there,
sir. She's like dead but she's not dead. She just lies.
She's been there maybe fourteen hours. We can't talk to
her.'

'Can you just forget her?'

'He's worth twenty million, sir. The husband.'

'Any idea the matter?'

'An Englishman left her, sir.'

'Ha,' said the owner after a pause. 'The guards will be there at eleven?'

'Yes, sir. But they can't carry her, sir. Not up the steps and over the dance floor. It's limbo night and we got the fire-eater. She's stiff as a board in a white bikini. We can't cart her through the tables. We got two High Court judges here to-night. Also it's the cabaret.'

'Could you make it look like the cabaret?'

'Not Mrs Santamarina, sir. She's no cabaret, sir. She's class. She's top class. She's cattle and grasslands, private aeroplane class. And she's lying on the beach, rings on every finger, sir. She's stiff as a board on the beach like a corpse. We can't get her off neither by sea nor land, sir.'

'Why not?'

'Well.' The manager paused. 'You can't get anyone much down on the beach after dark because of that nonsense, sir.'

'The murder?'

'Yessir.'

'For Godsake! Fifty years ago!'

'Yessir, but—no one would carry her through the glen, sir. Not even the guards later. No one would hardly go up near the beach at night even in a boat.'

'And the Englishman?'

'Gone two days ago to meet his wife at Kingston, sir.'

'Ha.'

'There might—'

'Yes?'

'There might be another guest, sir. Someone who didn't know about the beach at night. Or didn't mind.'

'Ah?'

'There's one of the judge's wives, sir. An Englishwoman. Would it be possible to ask?'

'My God yes. Ask her. Ask her fast. We want that damn

woman woken up, man. Fast. She'll be floating out to sea
next. We want no more trouble that beach.'

So, sidestepping Ned, bowing gracefully to the last of
the spring tycoons, the eel approached the judge's table
and asked if he might have a private word with Lady
Fletcher. A moment later she was taking her dignified way
to the beach, the manager beside her, down the steps to
the little bothy under the palms which hung like wings
to a stage. 'I will of course be within earshot,' he said and
vanished.

'But of course,' she replied, surprised for she could still
faintly hear the band above her in the trees. She smiled
up at him but found him gone.

Stepping out of the shadows on to the beach she thought,
'Well, *now* what?' and smiled. 'Whatever now?' she
thought.

The beach lay white as ever. Crabbed and crossed with
tracks, a photograph : black sea, black palms, white sand,
white moon, and quite deserted. The umbrellas were shut
up. The chairs slotted into each other, the far side of the
bay where the queer green house was, dark as midwinter
on a moor. There was nobody here.

Then she saw that two-thirds of the way across, a long,
bed-like object lay in the glare of the moon and on it a
long wooden creature with skull-holes for eyes and a great
length of limb pointed towards the sea. There, as dead,
dreadful under the moon lay Mrs Santamarina, most
decidedly alone.

Enid Fletcher walked carefully towards her on the nice
white shoes bought in Kingston and, reaching the long
creature, walked round her, chose a chair, shook it open
with one hand and sat upon it. Behind her was the glen
people kept away from, to one side of her the sea, to the
front of her the safe steps back up to the normal world.

There was also, on the sea side and a bit in front, something of a jetty and on it a couple of humps that might be people.

Lady Fletcher did not feel at all abandoned. She sat down heavily and slowly in the white chair and arranged her pretty, long skirt. She looked at the figure before her. It moved not a muscle. It gave no sign. The enamelled fingers, and toes, the finish and perfection of the effigy, suggested Egypt. The hair was a sculptured masterpiece. And the poor lady had been there all day.

Reasonable, practical queries rose in Lady Fletcher's mind. It must surely be time for her to move!

Of course, no food or drink. That might help. And the heat of the sun would have taken up moisture. But a remarkable mechanism none the less. And how thin she was. She probably ate and drank practically nothing anyway. And the sun is a great destroyer of time. You never do know how long you have been lying in the sun. How odd. The sun, the original clock, the only clock really : yet it can demolish time—wipe out what it was installed to create.

Perhaps sunstroke?

Lady Fletcher leaned forward and felt Monique Santamarina's pale brow. It was warm but not hot. She touched a hand, felt a pulse. There seemed no sign of fever. On the television and on films she had seen doctors push up an eye-lid to ascertain something or other, lean to the heart and listen. 'If I knew exactly what—' she thought.

But she didn't. And she didn't really feel in the least like leaning to or lifting any part of Mrs Santamarina. She had no medical knowledge and no experience of this sort of thing at all.

'And yet—and yet—' she thought.

'It's funny,' she thought, 'I'm quite sure of something.

I'm quite sure she is alive and well. Yes I am. I am as sure as I am that wherever we met, however much we saw of each other, this woman and I, in this world or the next, that we would not have one single thing in common.'

She sat on and after a while realised that there was something else she was sure of, too : that the woman was—whoever she was—suffering. And thus she took her hand.

'This woman suffering, ma'am,' said a voice and looking up she saw that a tall man had come apparently out of the sea and stood near her. He stood in the quiet sea up to his ankles—he had been one of the humps on the jetty. He wore only swimming trunks except for a chain and a medal round his neck. He was lithe and very tall. 'Somehow,' he said, 'she got to be got away.'

'I suppose,' said Lady Fletcher, 'you could carry her. Though I don't think they much want her to be carried across the dance floor up there. It's the cabaret. The manager says the fire-eater gets easily upset.'

The tall man walked out of the sea, dropped on his haunches and took hold of Mrs. Santamarina's other hand A glitter or two came from its fingers.

'And we can't take her through the glen apparently. It seems to be out of bounds.'

'She's not to go there,' said the man. 'I'll not carry her through there.'

'Couldn't someone come with a boat? Oh !' she cried, 'of course. I remember you. You are the man with the glass-bottomed boat. Couldn't you take her on board and we could take her round the point to—well, to a hospital or something?'

The boatman stroked Mrs Santamarina's hand and said, staring all the time at the shadows in her face and the great black glasses, 'No. Ma'am.'

'But we can't *leave* her,' said Lady Fletcher. 'We can't

leave her. And when the guards come on, whatever will they do? They look—well, not at all understanding. Those tin hats and rifles. They might . . .'

'That's right, ma'am.' The boatman sighed. 'They might fling her about, ma'am.'

The vision of Mrs Santamarina being flung about, perhaps frog-marched, even buffeted, up the steps, snarled at by the fire-eater, sneered at by the dancing girls, struck the two of them at the same moment as quite impossible.

'She must be saved,' said the boatman.

'Oh, but how?' said Enid Fletcher and squeezed the long bony hand.

A huge, astounding sigh broke from Mrs Santamarina, raising her magnificent chest then slowly, slowly, slowly deflating it, turning at last to a shudder which seemed to rack every part of her, every last Egyptian toe, and passed like a storm. The poor, long, marvellous, skinny body in its snippets of fifty-dollar bikini lay as before.

But the boatman was delighted. 'Go on,' he said, 'go on, missus.'

'Go on with what?'

'Well, say something now. Help her.'

'But how? I don't know what's the matter.'

'Git on now,' said the boatman.

'But I don't. I don't.'

'She's been left,' he said. 'He left her, the Englishman. The lawyer. He went to get his wife, Shaw.'

'Shaw?'

'That's the name. He left her.'

'Robert Shaw?'

'The lawyer.'

'Oh *dear*,' said Lady Fletcher and let go Mrs Santamarina's hand, 'oh, dear, oh dear. I know the Shaws.'

'Look,' said the boatman, and he leaned over the long,

Bolivian, corpse-like, suffering torso, 'look. She's in love. The Englishman left her. He gone for his beautiful English wife, ma'am. Tell her.'

'Tell her what?'

'Tell her somethin', missus. You know what to tell her. Look, I'll go git some rum,' and he went as he came, quickly, through the shallow edge of sea beside the black palms then round out of sight towards the land end of the jetty.

Lady Fletcher looked at Mrs Santamarina and thought, 'Oh dear—the silly nonsense.' A week ago she would have added to herself, 'I really can't do with this sort of thing.' She would have stood up and said clearly to the beautiful, silly woman, 'Now come along. You must come along now. It's very late and you are beginning to look very much a fool as well as causing a lot of trouble to everybody. You are behaving like a schoolgirl and you must be at least thirty. At the very least, come along at once.' She might even have leaned over and given the perfect, marble shoulder a shake or (temptation!) the perfect, sculptured cheek a wallop. She might, if she had been confident enough, even have gone on her new high heels to the sea's edge and filled her hands with some of it and trickled it all down the Santamarina diaphragm. 'You are a tedious and inane woman,' she might have said.

Instead she thought, 'The boatman's right. She is suffering.

'He's right. It is suffering. It will pass. She has had it before. She will have it again. But while it is there it is a bad pain. It is suffering.

'When you think about it—' For quite a while she thought about it, 'when you think about it, love is very mysterious. One body—' she looked at the framework of bones and skin and nails and hair on the beach bed, 'one body yearning for the presence of another body. One other *particular* body. It's not animal exactly either. There are animals of course' (she thought vaguely of swans) 'rather spiritual sort of animals. When one swan dies,' she thought, 'the other one goes off and dies, too, so they say. Dies singing, I believe.

'I have never much cared for swans,' thought Lady Fletcher. 'And they must look rather ridiculous, singing, when you think about it. Perhaps the notes come out through those little holes in the top . . .'

Looking down again, she now regarded Mrs Santamarina's impeccable navel and had an urge to stick a mast in it—a tall mast, a sort of wand with a little silk flag on top; and, pushing the crown of Mrs Santamarina's head with her finger tips, to pilot the whole contraption gently down the beach and watch it sail away out to sea. She imagined the woman on the long bed in the shape of a narrow boat lifting and tossing, out and out into the ocean, becoming a twig, a speck, tipping and dipping, at last turning right over and swooping, sinking, drowning deeper and deeper among the coral reefs, the little gold and dark blue fishes, toppling down the coral crags and cliffs. Would anyone miss her? Would Robert Shaw for long?

Surprising herself she took hold of Mrs Santamarina's hand once more and staring rather regally up at the sky, said, 'I know Anne Shaw.'

She was rewarded by something or other happening. A movement of the head? Not quite. An opening of the mouth? Not quite. A gleam from the Yorick glasses? Well, not quite but nearly.

And nearly a word came forth. Nearly.

She went on. 'I know Robert Shaw. And Anne Shaw. I have known them for years. Robert was in my husband's chambers. He is one of the nicest, most attractive men I have ever met. A most, charming, delightful man and a perfect husband. And he's a brilliant lawyer. And great fun. And he's very much admired.'

Praise the beloved. I know that's right. Looking quickly down she noted however that nothing much had changed. The lips perhaps had parted a little. No more. Off we go again.

'Anne—' she began. And stopped. What could she say about Anne? What is comforting about a lover's wife? Plainness? A plain wife eases jealousy. Or does she? Beauty? A beautiful wife and of a hitherto perfect husband could mean it had been a triumph.

Yes—but he went back. That's the point. Plain or beautiful he went back to her. Better perhaps not to be in fact going back to any kind of wife but to his children? For the sake of the children? Robert Shaw the loving father? And those children really are rather nice, I remember—

But a quick look at the ice-chiselled face made her abandon this appeal.

'Let me think,' prayed Lady Fletcher. 'Let me get it right. Let me imagine. Let me *be* her. The fat husband with the sausage fingers, the talk of cattle—or is it coffee? The whizzing in aeroplanes, the lolling on yachts. Vodka and champagne and those awful gin things. Parties, spick and span children hazy behind nursery-maids. Never a thing to do. How can I show her that her life overlaps with Robert Shaw's as much as mine with—the Duke of Edinburgh's? And he could no more run off with her than his wife, poor Anne, could run off with, well, with Lewis.'

'Blonde,' said Mrs Santamarina suddenly.

Thrown off her guard, Lady Fletcher jumped almost into the air. She had actually been laughing to herself at

E

the thought of Lewis and Anne Shaw (Could she have raised such an image in Wimbledon!), Lewis pouncing, glasses crooked, Anne saying, 'Oh, Judge! Goodness! What a surprise. Do have some coffee. I get it in Soho.'

'Blonde?' came the slow, throaty whisper again from the bier.

'I beg your pardon?'

'The wife is a blonde?'

Lady Fletcher speaking slowly, and silently requesting God to see that she didn't go wrong, said, 'Yes.

'Yes, his wife is a sort of blonde, I suppose. Yes. It's rather more *brown* hair than blonde, I think. Just a little faded perhaps. But she is a very pretty, nice girl—nearly forty now I suppose—in a very English sort of way. We age rather slowly, you know. It's the rain. She's a very—open—sort of girl, my dear. And very, well, innocent and d'you know I don't believe in a million years she might dream that her husband might look at another woman.'

Under the black glasses Lady Fletcher imagined she caught a gleam.

'Yes—I know you will find that hard to believe,' she said, 'in your world. But it is honestly quite true. There are thousands and thousands of people who never dream that their husbands and wives would ever look at anyone else. In England, I mean. Well actually in Scotland, too, I suppose, and perhaps in Wales. I haven't been to Ireland. I have thought about this a good deal lately for one reason and another. Since I was ill and came here, right away from Europe, I have had to think about it more. I do believe, dear, that we do get tremendously caught up in *work*—I mean intellectual work—in England. I believe that Oxford and Cambridge are very passionate places, and of course there's a lot of intellect there : but, particularly in the professions, if you are really *intellectually* busy—I don't mean a Crime practice—then I do think that relationships to do with sex do tend to get rather *slow*. After a time. Do you see, dear? Then, when we go abroad we get rather swept away. The English on cruises—they say it's the vibrations of the engines, but . . . And here of course it is the sun . . . But at home! My dear, at home Robert Shaw is working each night till midnight. Anything other than a wife—well, it would practically kill him.

'It's a life,' she went on, still looking at the sky. 'it's a life Anne has been brought up to—she's a lawyer's daughter. But you . . .'

'Blonde?' again said Mrs Santamarina.

'You don't understand. What she looks like doesn't matter. It's like a job being married to a top lawyer—I mean, *keeping* being married to him. You just sit there half the time. Doctors' wives have to put up with it, too. And it's'—Lady Fletcher swallowed hard because the bad bit was coming—'it's something they don't really want different. The husbands.'

The black orbs turned in the moonlight in Lady Fletcher's direction and Lady Fletcher said, looking straight at them, 'He won't leave her.' She said, 'He won't leave her. Some would. Some do. Even some as obsessed by his work as Shaw. But Shaw won't. He won't ever forget you. You will be like some—rainbow, or dream. But whatever she is like when he sees her again, whatever she looks like or behaves like, he'll stay with her. You had better realise and accept this now. Pretend that it is like a natural law—like Physics or Dynamics. Or even Chemistry, though that is a term that is very misused at present. It is the only way for you. HE WILL NOT LEAVE HER.'

The orbs did not shift from Lady Fletcher's face. 'Blonde?' said the Bolivian lips again and Lady Fletcher let go her hand and suddenly thumped both fists on sturdy knees, knees which had moved so squarely and heroically about Wimbledon Common for so many years.

'She is *not* blonde,' she cried, 'but don't you see? That is not what is at stake.'

Mrs Santamarina rose from her white hearse all in one long beautiful movement and without a sign of stiffness or unsteadiness began to move away across the beach. She reached the steps and began to climb them gracefully, and gracefully and looking most wonderfully expensive she had picked her way through the tables of the diners and across the milky marble dance floor before Lady Fletcher puffing slightly had even reached the top.

On she went, Mrs Santamarina, gliding past the band who pretended unsuccessfully not to see, gliding like a panther past the limbo dancers, past the cabaret girls, making them look like tarts, gliding beneath the molten nose of the fire-eater. A maid hurried forward and slipped a white beach robe over her shoulders and she disappeared towards her room beneath the colonnades.

The boatman appeared from behind a bush, like a chorus, clutching a bottle of rum, and said to Lady Fletcher, 'You did it, ma'am, you saved and cured her,' but Lady Fletcher only looked at him and nodded.

She felt rather tired. She walked carefully round the outside of the tables to their own secluded alcove and found Lewis and their friend the Jamaican judge talking earnestly together, hardly as if, she thought, I've been away.

'I wonder how long I have been away? Dear me, I feel odd. There is something funny about that beach. Something curious seems to happen to the time. How the land presses down against it, the weight and the mass of the trees in the slope behind, cutting off the world.'

The manager came up with orchids and a bottle of

wine. 'You are a miracle, my lady!' But she felt bewildered. In the distance across the dance floor the fire-eater gulped at his flames. She sat quietly on. Something strange and heavy like a flying grey lobster droned by her face. Heavy flowers, warm dark branches, sweet thick scents of night leaned to her, hung in the air. 'I have had enough,' she thought, and heard Lewis's voice and the Jamaican voice carefully answering it. 'Talking Law,' she thought. 'Law and order. I love order.

'Home on Thursday,' she thought. 'I shan't quite have missed the spring.' She was astonished at the violence of her delight.